book one of the silver sequence

the silver child

cliff mcnish

Carolrhoda Books, Inc. / Minneapolis

First American edition published in 2005 by Carolrhoda Books, Inc.
Published by arrangement with Orion Children's Books, a division of Orion Publishing
Group Ltd., London, England

Copyright © 2005 by Cliff McNish

Front cover photograph copyright © Michael Prince/CORBIS

The right of Cliff McNish to be identified as the author of this work has been asserted.

Carolrhoda Books, Inc.
A division of Lerner Publishing Group
241 First Avenue North
Minneapolis, MN 55401 U.S.A.

Website address: www.carolrhodabooks.com

Library of Congress Cataloging-in-Publication Data

McNish, Cliff.
        The silver child / by Cliff McNish.—1st American ed.
            p. cm.
        Summary: Drawn to a wasteland of garbage dumps called Coldharbour, six children
    undergo mysterious transformations and band together to face an unknown enemy.
        ISBN: 1–57505–825–1 (lib. bdg. : alk. paper)
        [1. Metamorphosis—Fiction. 2. Fantasy.] I. Title.
    PZ7.M239Si 2005
    [Fic]—dc22   2004012407

Manufactured in the United States of America
1 2 3 4 5 6 – BP – 10 09 08 07 06 05

For my dad, Eric McNish,
who really knew how to tell a story

contents

feast

MILO

No one could have eaten as much as Milo ate that afternoon.

It was Sunday lunch, and as usual the smells of cooking had given everyone an appetite—but surely nobody expected Milo to eat it all.

He and his younger sister, Jenny, were sitting at the table. Jenny twiddled her doll, while their mum brought out the food. There was more than enough for everyone: a large chicken, potatoes, bread fresh from the oven, roasted vegetables. A cheer went up from Jenny as Mum, swaying slightly under the load, brought out bowls of green beans and sweet corn.

It was a fantastic selection, almost a feast. A hungry man, if he had prepared himself, starved himself all day for just this one meal, might have been able to finish it off on his own. He might.

Milo started eating as soon as the last plate was laid

out. He began moderately enough, taking only a small piece of chicken and a couple of potatoes. "Mm," he said, grinning at Mum. He poured himself some water and took a sip. Reaching for a slice of bread, he put it neatly on the side of his plate for later.

Jenny fixed her own napkin and did her best to serve herself using the heavy spoons. She asked her doll if it wanted anything to eat. Some gravy, perhaps? Reaching for the gravy jug, she accidentally spilled her orange drink. With a resigned sigh, Mum went to the kitchen for a cloth.

When she came back, Milo's plate was empty. During the few seconds she had been away he had sneaked his hand across the table to take the bowl of potatoes. Calmly he ate them all, then started on the bread. At first no one paid any attention. Mum was still busy cleaning up, while Jenny hadn't yet decided what her doll wanted to eat. Meanwhile, Milo finished off the green beans, licked his fingertips and looked around for something else.

Seeing that there was no more food within easy reach, he got up from his chair and went round to the other side of the table. He came back with the bowl of sweet corn. It was a big bowl; he had to use both hands to lift it.

Mum glanced up. "And where do you think you're taking that?"

Milo didn't answer. He ladled several spoonfuls of corn onto his plate. Then, to save time, he started putting the corn from the bowl directly into his mouth.

"Milo!" snapped Mum. "For goodness sake!"

Jenny gave him a disgusted look, and laughed. "Pig!"

"Put that down," Mum said.

Milo ignored them both. The spoon had begun to irritate him. It was awkward, too slow. He threw it down and, lifting the bowl up to his mouth, used his fingers to shovel the tender corn past his lips.

"Ugh!" shouted Jenny. "Mum, look!"

"Milo!" Mum reached out for the bowl, attempting to take it out of his hands.

Jenny said, "Who's a greedy? Who's a greedy pig-piggy?"

Milo would not let go of the bowl. "Give that to me!" Mum demanded, fighting him for it. "Really, Milo . . . what's got into you? Put it down!"

"Piggy!" squealed Jenny.

Milo finished the sweet corn, then released the bowl. Mum, who had been clutching it tightly, staggered and nearly fell. Milo did not notice. He only saw the food. He stared longingly at the end of the table, where the rest of the bread and vegetables were waiting. The most efficient way to get at them was to yank the tablecloth towards him, so he did. Plates, glass and cutlery went everywhere. During the uproar that followed, Milo rapidly drew all the remaining food towards him. Indiscriminately, using alternate hands, left and right, he reached out. Without looking at the food—without even attempting to taste it any longer—he stuffed whatever was nearest into his mouth.

"Milo . . . Milo will you *stop*!" shouted Mum. "What are you doing?"

Jenny started to cry—orange fizz had spilled on her doll. When Milo snatched the doll and licked its cloth face experimentally, she shrieked and kicked him under the table.

Milo threw the doll down. He was seeking a faster way to consume. His teeth felt suddenly in the way. His tongue was too thick, his jaw lacking the flexibility he wanted it to possess. He opened his mouth as wide as possible. Then, grunting with the effort, he forced it even wider, testing the limits of the jawbone. Did he have to chew? Did he have to waste time doing that? Thrusting his head back, Milo tried pouring the food down his throat, using his teeth as little as possible—just enough so that the food did not catch and make him gag as it made its way down.

"Milo!" gasped Mum. She tried to grasp both his hands, but with extraordinary energy he twisted away from her.

There was no bread left, but the margarine was available. Milo dug his fingers into it. Avoiding his teeth, he pushed the margarine deep inside his throat. His breathing was heavy and he did not look up.

Mum made another attempt to stop him. This time she wrapped both her arms around his body. "What are you doing?" she sobbed, pulling him to the carpet. Milo screeched. He flailed his arms and broke free of Mum again.

She lay on the floor, a hand across her chest, afraid of him.

"Drink," Milo rasped. "Drink. Drink." He reached under the table, finding a half-spilled can of lemonade. Placing the can directly over his mouth, he squeezed hard. Most of the liquid fell down his chin and splashed onto the carpet. Milo didn't care; it was quicker to drink this way than any other. As soon as the can was empty, he picked up another, finishing the entire contents without taking a breath. The only drink left belonged to Jenny.

"No!" His sister was too young to understand the full strangeness of what was taking place. She struggled with him for the drink. Milo ripped it away from her and swallowed as if his mouth was a desert.

Mum, getting to her feet, knocked the can out of his hand. When he went to pick the can up, she held his wrists again. "What's got into you?" she shouted. "Stop . . . stop fighting me!"

Milo freed himself, stood up and pushed the table over. The half-eaten chicken, the last item of food remaining, fell by his feet. He picked it up. It was an awkward shape to get into his mouth. He turned it this way and that, finding the best way to squeeze the flesh past his teeth.

There were tears in Mum's eyes. "What are you doing?" she yelled. "Milo, look at me! Look at me!"

Milo scuttled to a corner of the room. He still had the chicken. He sat in the corner, eating it steadily. Jenny ran across to Mum and hid against her dress. Milo warily watched them, as if at any moment they would attempt to steal the chicken. Mum approached him cautiously.

"What's wrong?" she asked, in the softest of voices. "Milo, it's all right. It's all right. What's wrong? Please tell me . . ."

Milo glanced up. Just for a second he appeared to recognize her. He stopped chewing. He looked at his filthy hands. He felt the stickiness and mess over his face and neck. He saw his sister staring at him, terrified.

Then something happened to his eyes. They changed. They *bulged*. A force behind the eyeballs distinctly squeezed them and made them push outward. It was such an abnormal movement that even his mum recoiled.

Milo touched his eyelids. They were warm. His blue irises expanded and contracted under them. There was a rhythm to the motion, like a pulse, like an engine.

Mum reached out her hand to him. For a moment Milo looked up at her and accepted that hand. He let her put it against his cheek. "Oh Milo . . ." she murmured, ". . . what's happening to you?"

He trembled. "Mum, I . . . I don't know."

Her hand reached his hair. She stroked it gently. As she did so a few of Milo's blond curls fell onto her fingers and dropped to the floor. More hair followed, every part she touched. She withdrew her hand. A great tuft came away on her fingers, leaving the skin above Milo's left temple exposed.

Jenny screamed.

"Let me help you," Mum said.

"I don't know what I need," Milo croaked.

She moved towards him again, but Milo backed away. "Don't be afraid," she said.

Milo stood up unsteadily—as if he half-expected even this simple action to be suddenly beyond him. He lurched to the front door, all the while dragging his fingers across his scalp. By the time he had opened the door there was no hair remaining on the left side of his head.

"Don't leave," Mum pleaded. "Where are you going?"

"I can't stay," he said. "I think . . . I think this is only the beginning."

"The beginning of what?"

"I don't know."

Jenny stared at Milo. She watched the strands of his hair drifting to the floor. Catching one, she turned it slowly in the light coming through the window.

Milo stood at the front door, the sun warming the bald part of his head. He wiped his chicken-smeared hand on his shirt, quickly stepped outside and shut the door.

Mum cut across the room, reaching for the handle. Wrenching it open, she ran outside. The street was empty. She shielded her eyes, dazzled by the afternoon sun. In the distance, she could just make out the estuary and the grim flatness of Coldharbour beyond.

Milo was gone.

coldharbour

THOMAS

"We always come here to play, Thomas."

A six-year-old girl told me that, the first morning I arrived in Coldharbour.

Susie, her name was. I learned a lot from that wise little girl in the brief period she befriended me. She showed me around—took my arm in a protective, almost motherly way. Looking back, I think she just felt sorry for me. I'm not surprised. What a pathetic sight I must have been: a rich boy from the suburbs, holding a carrier bag of food, stumbling about in Coldharbour without a clue.

Coldharbour! What a flat wilderness of derelict steel and muck! Susie told me that ships were built here once. I found that hard to believe. All you could see of the old shipyards by the time I arrived were a few girders and broken-into warehouses nobody had bothered to dismantle. Apart from that there was only mud, miles and miles of the stuff extending out to the sea.

Kids got lost in Coldharbour. Susie told me that, and I believed her. It was such a vast, desolate place. And it stank, too! After the shipbuilders left, huge refuse dumps had been constructed around its borders to take the rubbish from the nearest towns. Depending on the direction of the wind, all that rubbish came blowing across the flats, chasing off the seagulls and fouling up the air. Sometimes the smell was so bad that even the gangs covered their noses as they went about their business.

If anyone ran Coldharbour now, it was the child-gangs. This was a good place for them to operate, I suppose: virtually deserted, and not too far from the nearest towns. Plenty of room, too, to set up territories, give chase, hide or hang out.

But the gang kids just came for fun, didn't they? They came for a lark about. And they were fairly safe because they moved around in big groups.

I was on my own. What was *I* doing here? What on earth had driven me here and kept me in this frightening place? I had no idea. Not lack of love, certainly. My parents loved me. I knew that. Their love waited only a few days' walk away. I could have left the muck of Coldharbour and been tucked up in my warm old bed in a twinkling.

So why hadn't I gone back? I had no idea. I didn't even know why I'd left home in the first place. I remember this: waking at dawn, and staring out of my window. I was staring in the direction of Coldharbour, but I didn't know that then. I couldn't even see the place from my house; I'd barely heard of it. But as I gazed raptly out, I had no doubt. I knew that in Coldharbour something remarkable was waiting for me.

It made no sense, but two minutes later I was closing the front door behind me. I didn't even think to leave a note, or bring my cell phone. With no idea what I was doing, I traveled vaguely south. I walked for days, eating from my carrier bag, avoiding all major roads and sleeping in quiet places in the countryside. Why? Because I knew my parents would be looking for me. Police search parties were bound to be everywhere. If they found me, they'd make me go back home. I couldn't risk that. Whatever secret awaited me in Coldharbour was too important.

Dumb rich boy. That's what the gang kids called me, when I arrived in my giveaway clothes. And those first kids I met scared me so much that almost every night I'd think of setting off back home. "Hi, Mum! Hi, Dad!" I'd picture myself saying, as my hand rapped on the door.

I did start back too, several times, but never got far. Whatever drew me to Coldharbour, kept me here. I couldn't explain it. I didn't leave my parents completely wondering what had happened to me, of course. I had a bit of change and phoned from the edge of Coldharbour to let them know I was okay. I didn't say where I was, though. I couldn't risk them finding me.

Coldharbour! What a bleak setting! I'd expected

whatever drew me here to show up the moment I arrived, but I was wrong. I'd walked all this way to be greeted only by dirty-looking seagulls and emptiness. As I stumbled nervously around, I couldn't believe how barren and unwelcoming a place Coldharbour was. Find a way to survive if you can, it seemed to be saying. Make a home if you dare!

Susie saved me, really. She taught me how to keep my head down, avoid the more dangerous gangs. When she wasn't around, I didn't have a clue. It was summertime, or I'd never have got through those first nights. Dumb rich boy; the gangs were right about that, and initially I spent most of my time skulking in doorways at the outer limits of Coldharbour just trying to hide from the more scary-looking kids, and quietly starving.

Food. Let me tell you about food. After I'd gone only one day without any, it was all I could think about. The carrier bag's worth of stuff I'd taken with me from home didn't even last the journey, and I'd been in too much of a rush to think of bringing more than a few coins. That left me in a nasty situation. There was only one source of nourishment in Coldharbour—the food dumps. If I was going to stay, I had no choice other than to start looking for meals there. At first I couldn't. The idea of digging around in someone's old scraps was too disgusting. I refused to even consider it. But I learned something quickly in Coldharbour: hunger's a funny old fellow; he'll make you weep; he'll drive you to do almost anything.

After a couple of days with nothing to eat it was amazing how fast I changed my mind about visiting the refuse dumps. Food scraps started looking much more palatable. The fresher stuff actually started looking good! Leftovers became my friend!

I wasn't the only kid scavenging here, either. There were some poor families living on the margins of Coldharbour who sent their kids daily to scrap on the dumps. They didn't come for food, of course—none of them were as desperate as me. They came for dumped household items: discarded fridges, radios, broken TVs, anything really that could be salvaged or traded. These kids were experts. It was almost a pleasure to watch them at work. Once I saw a girl pluck out a pair of nearly new suede boots from a grubby bag I'd never even have seen. A few had been coming here for years, and had perfected a peculiar crab-like way of scrambling over the dumps, taking their time to avoid stepping on anything sharp. I followed them from a distance, learning the technique, and applying it to the food dumps.

Three weeks. It took me that long to make myself a rubbishy home in a derelict warehouse, and get in well enough with one of the bigger gangs to be left alone. Susie helped there. I'd have been lost without that special girl. The gang she belonged to let me live close to the southeast dump in relative safety.

"But what are you doing *staying* here every night?" Susie kept asking me. "You're mad! You must be mad!

Only the biggest gangs leave anyone here at night, and never on their own."

I couldn't answer her. Maybe I *was* mad—an insane boy. Why not? I began to think so. Wasn't it mad to wait endlessly for something to turn up in this desolate place? Wasn't that, after all, exactly the sort of thing a crazy person might do?

All I knew for certain was that apart from being hungry all the time, I was scared. My new warehouse home scared me most of all. An abandoned warehouse is a frightening place at night, let me tell you. It wasn't so much the dark as the animals. Rodents mostly. I couldn't keep them out because the warehouse's iron doors simply would not shut. I spent days, just trying to close those doors! For a while my entire life was focused on it.

Despite this, after only a week or so I had a sort of daily routine established. In the morning, after chasing out the rodents, I'd head straight for the dumps. Because I wasn't any good at finding food, I usually spent all day looking for it. Evening would creep up on me eventually, and then, if I was lucky, I might get a sunset. Sunset over the rubbish dumps: a strange sight, but useful, because when the sun is low it glints better on metal foil and plastic wrappings containing food. After a last scavenge in the dying light, I'd head back to the warehouse, to be greeted by whatever four-legged guests fancied dropping by. Then—darkness. I dreaded the nights, I really did. When you are genuinely hungry, when you haven't eaten properly for days, you can't sleep. It's impossible. And I was always freezing, too. I'd lie there, my stomach gnawing at me, shivering under a dirty edge of canvas, trying not to listen to the animals scurrying about.

What on earth was I doing here!

I think it was in my second week that I began to hear a noise. Not the sound of kids, or the skittery-squeak of animals; I was used to those. This noise was entirely different. It was like a distant roar. Why I called it that I couldn't say, but all night I would hear that roar. And in the dawn it would still be there underlying the singing of birds, and endlessly, throughout the day, when it was quiet enough, I would hear it.

A month. That's how long I waited in my cozy new home with my mouse and rat friends, growing steadily filthier and skinnier in Coldharbour. And every night I'd look up through the high broken windows of the warehouse, still expecting to see something remarkable. Perhaps a wondrous blotting out of stars. Perhaps someone who would drag open the heavy doors and show me the reason I was here.

But I saw nothing, and the arrival of each day brought the same dreary routines. The truth was that I'd found a way to exist in Coldharbour, but that's literally all I was doing—scrapping along the dumps, trying to keep myself together while avoiding the worst of the gangs.

And then, one morning, I felt compelled to go north. I left all the hard-won safety of my warehouse behind, and on some mad impulse carried my canvas blanket to a place nearer the river estuary. I didn't know this part of Coldharbour at all. Here I had nothing: no place to stay, no food, no rights negotiated with the gangs to be in their territories.

And then—well, then I met the twins.

I was scavenging as usual that morning. Without being too conspicuous, I'd brought all the food I could carry with me as I headed north. After it ran out, I had to take my chances with the unknown gangs cruising around the north dumps. Actually, this was my second visit there. The first time three lads had chased me off with a warning. The next time I entered their territory I knew I could expect a beating. Nothing personal—they just didn't want anyone they didn't know in their territory, as simple as that. But hunger never leaves you alone for long. So, the very next morning, there I was again, tramping around the dump like an idiot, hoping I wouldn't be seen. I chose dawn this time. The refuse lorries didn't usually turn up till later in the day, so it was the safest hour to scavenge.

When I arrived there were only a few others around. Most were single kids, hoping for something that might have been left late yesterday on the household dumps. They watched with distaste as I passed by, making my way onto the closest food dump. I ignored their comments, and started sorting through the usual leftovers.

But when I saw the twins I stopped. Well, we all did.

Nobody looks quite normal wandering about in Cold-harbour's mud, but the twins made everyone stare.

They were the weirdest creatures I had ever seen. I didn't notice their faces at first, just the way they moved. Initially, I thought their motion was like an animal, until I realized it was stranger than that; they moved like insects. Each of them had skinny arms and legs that were thrust out sideways, beetle-fashion. They ran about that way, on all fours, their weight balanced on the tips of their toes and fingers, bodies low, bellies almost touching the ground.

As I approached, I heard them making little interested sounds and huffs.

Then they raised their faces, and I was shocked: they were girls, clearly twins. Identical-length thick red hair dangled over their bent knees as they turned this way and that. But here was the most shocking thing of all: every-thing about the way they moved should have made them appear grotesque, but oddly it didn't, because they were clean. Everyone in Coldharbour picks up a layer of grime within days—you can't avoid it—but the twins were spotless. They had freckles. You could see dimples. Pretty faces, too: delicate chins, slightly upturned noses, clear green eyes. I could almost imagine the same girls sitting at a dining table, politely unfolding their napkins.

But the way they moved! Gazing at them, I suppose they might have been half-ordinary girls once, but what were they now? They had surprisingly good white teeth, well maintained, none missing. I noticed those teeth straightaway because both girls were smiling. They were smiling—and looking right at me.

All the other kids nearby backed away. Scrapper kids aren't easily driven off, but what were these scary things? I started to retreat, too, but as I did so the twins made a noise like a whelp. With difficulty, as if they had nearly forgotten how, they stood upright. They raised themselves up and just stood there more humanly, wavering a little, looking directly at me as if I ought to be impressed.

I saw then what they were wearing: dresses, or the remains of them. Yellowish ones, the same kind, with small pink flowers, as if at one time a proud mother had wanted to show them off. Whatever attractiveness those clothes had once possessed was long gone. The dresses were clean enough, but such a patchwork of repairs! The girls, however, obviously didn't care what I thought of their clothes. Both of them were smiling cheerfully at me, their hands pressed together, hugging each other.

Without taking my eyes off them, I took a few steps back. The twins glanced at each other. Then they dropped again on all fours—and ran at me.

God, they were fast! Flattened out, scuttling on their fingertips and toenails, they reached me in seconds. None of the other kids came to help me, of course; not here. As the twins approached I stiffened, wanting to run, but how could I escape anything that moved so quickly? I decided to stay still, pulling in my arms in case they wanted a bite.

The twins circled me, nodding to each other, sniffing merrily away as if they'd found their mummy or something.

"Go away!" I shouted as loudly as I could. "I've got no food for you."

"You got food?" One of them was speaking. Can you believe it? Words.

"No," I insisted. "No food. I haven't got any. What do you think I'm doing here at the dump? No food." I emptied the pockets of my jeans.

One of the girls smiled mischievously. "You ain't here for food," she said.

"No, you ain't, matey," the other said. "Take uz 'ome wiv you."

"What?" I looked at them. They were grinning non-stop. One of the girls turned in a tight circle and whooped at a cloud.

"If I 'ad a tail, I'd be wagging away," she said.

"If I 'ad a rope, I'd go out and play," the other said.

Flipping heck! I thought. They had both settled at ease beside me, like lapdogs waiting for a lap. "Just let me go!" I said. "Get out of my way!" I looked round for a weapon—or a place to run.

"Take uz 'ome," one of the girls said again.

"What do you mean, home?" Would they be less likely to bite me if I talked to them? Or perhaps, after all, they just needed to be told where north and south were. "Are you lost, is that it?" I asked. "You lost out here? Can't find your own home?" And I couldn't help thinking: what outrageous family might they belong to? Even in Coldharbour, I couldn't imagine a gang that would have them.

The twins had tucked their feet under their dress rags. They were sitting on the balls of their feet, looking thoughtfully up at me.

One of them said, "If I 'ad an orange, I'd peel the skin."

The other said, "If I 'ad a nut, I'd suck it in."

I just looked at them like the crazy things they were. "Where is your home?" I asked, trying to get some sense out of them. "Do you live here, on the dump itself?" Then, very slowly, "Do—you—live—here?"

The twins seemed to find this hilarious. They started laughing and rubbing my feet with their fingers. "Take—uz—to—your—'ome," one of them copied me, as if I was a nitwit. She carefully formed the shape with her mouth. "*Your* home."

"My home? What?" I haven't got a home here, I thought—or not one I'd dare take you back to. The girls stayed beside me, clearly expecting something.

"We found 'im, all right," one said, kissing the other excitedly on the cheek.

"Found who?" I asked.

"Found *you*!" she hooted, slapping the ground. The other one hugged her, deliriously happy.

I had no idea what they were talking about, and at that

moment I was too scared to care. Obviously I couldn't outrun them, so what else could I do? They could speak at least. Keep chatting to them, I thought, until you can work out how to get away.

"What . . . are your names?" I asked.

They exchanged glances.

"Emily," one said, standing and taking a shaky bow.

"Freda," said the other, curtsying.

I gingerly held my hand out to shake theirs—keeping my fingers well away from their mouths.

"Pleased . . . to meet you, Emily and Freda," I said, trying to smile.

They grinned and shook formally back. After that we fidgeted a bit, like any other newly introduced people, and I wondered what to say next that would keep them calm. I couldn't think of anything. Then one of the girls put her hand on my leg and urged me in the gentlest of voices, "Go on, take uz 'ome wiv you. Go on."

"I haven't got a home here," I said.

Amazingly, she started crying. Then the other one joined in with her. They both put their thin hands over their eyes. "Take uz, please," they wailed, their whole bodies shuddering, arms around each other in a sisterly way.

I could see they weren't so dangerous now, but I was still afraid. I tried to step over them. When they clung to my legs I half-kicked them off, and, surprisingly, they let go. As I walked away both girls squealed, a piteous sound.

I strode off, looking back every few seconds. They came silently after me.

"Get lost!" I shouted, feeling bolder now.

They merely lowered their faces and continued to follow.

Other kids were watching us from the edges of the dump. Some of them had picked up sticks or taken out their personal weapons—just in case the twins decided to take an interest in them. I found a stone heavy enough to do some damage, turned around, and raised my arm. "You see this?" I yelled. "Clear off! Go on! Go back to wherever you came from!"

They just looked at me and smiled their smiles.

I strode away, and this time didn't look back for several minutes. All the while I could hear their stealthy, quick movements behind me. Eventually I stopped again. If I actually took them back to the place I'd slept the previous couple of nights, would I ever be rid of them? I showed them the stone. "This is my last warning!" I growled. When they continued to follow, I threw it. I missed—deliberately—and they laughed.

"Ah, poor laddie," one said. "If I'd a stone, I'd throw it better."

"If I'd a stick, I'd whack it harder," the other said.

Flipping lunatics! Everything I had learned in Coldharbour told me to keep away from them. "I'll do it!" I warned, picking up another stone and jabbing my arm forward. "I will!"

"Do it, then!" one of them wailed—and they dashed towards me.

I threw the stone, and this time in my panic I hit one of the girls on the shoulder. I expected her to run off—or maybe jump at me—but do you know what she did? She just looked at me, her lips quivering. "Take uz 'ome!" she begged, her big eyes wide and solemn. "You do it. You takes uz wiv you." They both stared at me as if I was the fount of all human kindness, as if I couldn't possibly have meant to harm them.

"We ain't going away!" the one called Freda said, her voice shaking with emotion. "Chuck your stones, but we ain't leaving!"

I looked at them both, their belly buttons pressed to the ground, skinny arms and legs pointing trembling through their dress-ends, and realized something at last—they were as frightened as me of this place.

I stood there, my hands shaking.

The girls, encouraging each other, skittered closer. I raised my arm halfheartedly to hit them—but I couldn't. How could I? And suddenly I felt something new for them: not fear, but pity. I felt a bit of pity. And that's when I discovered the beginning of my gift. I felt it seep out of me and into them, just a trickle. I didn't know what it was that first time, but I would later, when the twins explained it to me in their own way. It was a kind of beauty. That's what they called it. Beauty. A comfort. Like everything the twins wanted or needed at that very moment: a feeling of security, of being accepted, of fire-side warmth, of belonging. Someone who looked after them.

Family.

And I just stood there amazed. I didn't understand what had happened. All I knew was that some small portion of my mind had gone into the twins—and whatever it was, they had been waiting for it. Afterwards, I just lingered at the edge of the dump, with a dab of rain starting up, surrounded at a distance by gang kids blinking at me, and with these two girls, snuffling and emotional and suddenly contented, nuzzling their faces against my legs, and all I could think was, "What am I?"

THREE

the coolness of water

MILO

Milo staggered away from home, holding the side of his head.

In the last hour most of his hair had fallen out. A single clump remained near his ear. Or was he holding it on? Yes, he was—his hand held it there. He removed his fingers and the last strands fell off, scattering and drifting away on the wind.

I'm not scared, he realized. Shouldn't I be scared? Surely I should be scared! But he felt no fear whatsoever. He stopped to feel his scalp, exploring the bumps that had always been hidden. The smoothness was astonishing: like something unreal, not his head at all.

What are you doing? he thought. This is ridiculous! Go back home. Mum'll be worried sick. It's not fair to her. But he wasn't ready to return home yet. Without understanding why, a terrific exhilaration drove him to run and run and run.

Finally he stopped. His feet had carried him up several streets. He went to the highest point of land overlooking the town and gazed around.

What was he looking for?

His new eyes guided him. They had undergone further changes. Each one could now rotate in separate directions. Milo felt awed as he set them loose, to decide for themselves where they wished to look. Both eyes swiveled northwards, towards the fields that opened out beyond the town. There was an isolated farmhouse in that direction.

Something drew Milo there, and he ran towards it.

When he arrived, uncertain what to do next, he hid outside under the kitchen window. A man's voice was coming from inside the house—a dad speaking to his daughter. Milo found himself listening to the girl's voice. He heard her name. Helen. Her name was Helen. For a few minutes he simply crouched under the window, fascinated by her.

There was a special quality about this girl, but what?

He listened to her for a little longer, trying to unlock the secret. Then he ran in confusion from the house. What was he supposed to do now? More changes were about to take place inside him. Milo sensed them, without knowing what they would be. I have to get through the remainder of the day, he thought. I have to find somewhere to stay. Where can I go? Where should I go to be safe?

His eyes tugged him south. They plotted a path towards the river, showing him the muddy spaces of Coldharbour beyond. Coldharbour? Why there? With the remarkable things happening to him, surely Coldharbour was the last place he could expect help if he needed it. Even so, Milo trusted his eyes and headed steadily that way.

When he reached the river, he made for an empty stretch of the bank. For a while he simply lay there, feeling his body changing in subtle ways. Then the hunger pangs returned. It was the same pressing need to eat that had overwhelmed him in the dining room at home.

But there's no food here, he thought desperately. There's nothing!

He was wrong. His eyes had drawn him to the one location where there was enough to satisfy his appetite— the food dumps of Coldharbour. Milo lurched towards the nearest dump. His improved eyes discovered food in places other children would never have found it. For nearly an hour he gorged himself out of boxes and packets and bags. He did not stop until the gnawing pain ended. Afterwards he opened his mouth and drank from the river, a long, long draught. Then he waited for something to happen.

Nothing.

Some time passed. Twilight, the sky deepened, and Milo hid from a group of girls wandering along the bank of the river. Later, when it was quiet again, he came back to the water and stared at his reflection.

A bald-headed boy stared back at him.

Milo smiled. He felt mysteriously unafraid of this new boy.

On impulse he dangled his hands in the river. His skin was unusually warm, and the cold water felt good. Kneeling, Milo slowly pushed his arms all the way under. His shoulders followed. He had an irresistible urge to go further—to lower his head. He did so. First his lips and nose. Then, holding his breath, his entire face. He kept his eyes open. The sensation of the water passing across them was pleasant, and he left them submerged in the river for several minutes.

Eventually, with water dripping from his chin, Milo lifted his face and gazed out over the town again. It was different. At first he could not understand in what way, until he saw the children. To Milo, each child now shone like a patch of light. They were a creamy white, while the everyday world around them was a duller gray. And there were thousands of them. Before he had only been able to pick out a few gang kids traipsing in and out of Coldharbour, but now Milo could see each child with absolute clarity for miles around. Even those inside their homes were visible—nothing, not even doors and walls could hide them from him.

A gray world shining with children. Each child vibrant, sharp-edged, glowing like a flare. Milo glanced up and the sun seemed pale beside them. It was as if from now on the only objects meaningful to his eyes would be those beating with a child's fast heart.

He turned to survey all those in Coldharbour and the nearest towns. Then he drew himself to his full height and raised his arms. For some reason he wanted all the children to approach him. He expected them to. Couldn't they see him? How could he make them see him?

He searched for his own home. It was a speck hidden behind hills in the far distance—but not to Milo's eyes, because Jenny's patch of light was there. He saw her. She was standing at her bedroom window, looking forlornly outward. There was a darker area in her left hand, the shape, he realized, of her doll.

That evening a strengthening breeze blew across the unprotected river flats, cooling Milo's eyes further. He breathed deeply, watching the world.

Night arrived, and with it, on the other side of the river, a gang of menacing-looking kids emerged from Coldharbour. A couple of them noticed him and shouted loudly. When Milo did not reply, they started making their way towards the nearest bridge to get across to him.

FOUR

beauty

THOMAS

Me and the twins. One boy, two insect-girls: my wacky new family!

Emily and Freda looked so bizarre I thought I'd never feel at ease in their company, but I was wrong. They took one glance at the filthy shed I'd been staying in the last few nights and almost died with embarrassment for me.

"C'mon," Freda said. "You ain't much good at constructing stuff, Toms. Emms and me will 'ave to take you in hand."

And they did. At incredible speed the twins fixed us up a sort of—well, home would be to dignify it. It was a shack, really, planks and sticks pinned down with rope, hung over with a piece of old tarpaulin they nicked and dragged from a building site a few miles west.

Our new home. It was such a nothing of a home really, but the twins were entirely happy when we were inside. It was as if their whole purpose in life was fulfilled by sharing this manky shack with me. I was amazed by how quickly we settled down together. The twins taught me how to stay clean in a world of muck. They proved companionable, too, with their wonky little rhymes, and hardly seemed to need a thing of their own.

When we required things, they foraged. There are no shops in Coldharbour, but the twins could sniff out food on a dump faster than any kid I'd seen. I was well fed, the twins saw to that. For the first time in weeks I even had some luxuries. The girls found extra clothes, so I could change sometimes. They discovered a soft, not-bad mattress. They got me a pillow and a couple of ropy old sheets. Somewhere they picked up a flashlight that actually worked, and at night we'd huddle together and read a magazine or newspaper that had blown off one of the dumps, or just sit in the dark listening to the unsettling winds of Coldharbour.

As for my beauty—my gift—I examined myself at quiet times for its purpose, but it never appeared to mean anything more than offering a bit of warmth to the twins. I continued to do that, giving them a flutter of beauty every now and again. And in return, I suppose, they fed me and kept me entertained. They also kept up their improvements to the shack, cozying things, fixing and tarting it up with plastic sheeting so that even when it rained heavily we barely felt a drip. And as they did so I kept thinking: where else except in Coldharbour could three children set up house together, and not be bothered by anyone? Was that why we had come here?

The shack wasn't even cramped. I noticed that there was plenty of room in it for three more to fit snugly—or one giant. Initially I thought the twins had created all that space purely for my benefit, but later I wondered.

"Why all this room?" I asked Freda one morning. "You expecting guests?"

She just gave me an inscrutable look, saying nothing.

"Dunno," she said, when I pressed her.

"Maybe," Emily added. Both girls stayed silent after that, which was unusual for the twins; normally they never stopped chatting for a second.

Not for the first time, I wondered what had driven the girls away from their home. Had they just walked away like me? Perhaps they'd been thrown out by terrified parents who'd caught them scampering about. Or— could they have been born this way?

"Were you . . . always like this?" I asked. "Did you get thrown out because of . . . " I indicated their hands and feet.

"No, it's recent," Freda said, glaring at me severely. "D'you think our mum would've chucked uz out for a little thing like this? You don't know her! Mum was scared, but she never would've loved uz any less 'cause of this!"

Chastened, I said nothing for a while.

Emily gazed at me, filled with exasperation. "Don't you know? Don't you even know yet why we're here? We came for you! We 'ad to find yer."

"We 'ad to treasure and mind yer," Freda said.

"What?" I frowned. "But I discovered *you*. On the dumps, remember."

Freda shook her head, clearly amused. "We'd been shivering, waiting for you to turn up on that flipping rubbish heap so long we was almost starving ourselves," she said. "Gawd, we'd been searching days."

"Why?"

"Dunno, Toms." She glanced thoughtfully at me. "We're here to find 'em, we think—special ones like you. You're the first. Emms reckons our noses need to improve before we're ready to find the others."

"What others?" I asked.

"Dunno," Emily replied. "If we knew, there'd be no delay."

"If we knew, we'd be up and away," Freda said.

I stared uncertainly at them both. Then I looked up at the ceiling. As always, I could hear the ever-present noise of the sound I called the roar. It was like an endless wind brushing past our roof. I wondered if the girls could detect it, too. I'd been scared to ask them, it unnerved me so much.

"Emily . . . Freda . . . " I whispered, ". . . can you hear anything?"

I think it must have been the way I said it that made the twins react so strongly. Both sat upright. Then, urging each other on, neither wanting to be the first to start, they pursed their lips. The sound that emerged made me back away from them because it was a perfect rendition of the roar. I had once tried myself to imitate the sound when I was alone, but it took two voices working together to produce it accurately. It was terrifying. The girls stopped immediately, as fearful as me, overcome with emotion.

"What is it?" I rasped. "Do either of you understand?"

They shook their heads—but we all knew it was something dreadful.

"Other kids aren't able to hear it," I told them. "I've asked the gangs. They don't know what I'm talking about. Maybe . . . maybe only *we* can hear it."

Emily stared at me. "What are we part of, Toms?"

I knew then that the girls had no more idea than me. They edged closer and for a while we just sat there, looking at each other, our faces lit by sunshine coming through the gaps in the piece of wood we called our front door.

We were too frightened to speak any more about the roar that day. Instead we busied ourselves with little tasks into the evening, and the next morning there was food to find as usual. A couple of days later the twins went out. They returned with pens, envelopes, stamps and a few sheets of paper between their teeth.

"What's this for?" I asked.

"Write a letter home," Freda explained. "Family's important. Let 'em know you're okay, Tommy."

"Oh. I see."

The twins wrote their letters. It wasn't easy for them. Their hands had hardened with all the running; they could no longer properly hold a pen. Seeing them concentrating so hard on writing legibly, I felt strangely moved. These girls were just like me. Somewhere else they had another home and family they had once called their own. It was pitiful to watch them clumsily signing their names on the letters, small tears in their eyes, putting numerous kisses at the bottom—and adding more around the edges of the paper.

I wrote a letter afterwards to my own parents. I felt awful about what I was putting them through—of course I did—but ever since I'd first heard the roar I felt more compelled than ever to stay in Coldharbour.

As soon as we finished writing, Emily and Freda stuffed the envelopes in their mouths and left to make the long journey to the nearest post box. When they returned they were subdued.

"What are we doing here?" I asked them. "It's ludicrous! Eating rubbish! Sitting in a shack scribbling letters! Why aren't we with our families? Shouldn't we be at home with them?"

Both girls nodded, but they made no move to leave. None of us did and, looking at their determined expressions, I began for the first time to understand why. "It's the roar, isn't it?" I said. "The reason we're here has something to do with it. Whatever's making that sound is . . . *coming here.*" The girls stared fearfully at me, and I glanced up, listening. "It's too big for us to stop," I whispered. "When you listen to it, you can tell that. You can tell—"

"Shhh . . ." Emily gave me a tight smile. "I've got itchy feet."

"We're a family now," Freda added, "but we ain't complete."

"There's someone else coming to join us, you mean?" I said. "Someone . . . strong enough to fight this thing?"

"Dunno," Emily said, clutching hopefully at Freda's hand. "Wait and see."

The summer days moved on, and despite the specter of the roar my main concern was that another kid would report seeing the twins. Then no doubt police—or maybe zookeepers! Emily said—would take an interest in our lives. But we were lucky, and most of the time the twins were careful to stay off their hands when anyone else was nearby.

I thought the prospect of the roar would make me miserable, but the twins kept my spirits up, and their enthusiasm was contagious. After all the gloomy weeks of life on my own I felt almost secure with the girls. It was ridiculous because I even felt safe, and only a fool could feel truly safe in Coldharbour. Once our shack was homey enough, certain local gangs naturally started to take a keen interest in what we had, but Emily and Freda kept them away. People were scared of the twins—seeing a girl running on all fours faster than a dog can have that effect!

Midsummer arrived, and it was a peculiar time for me. Days passed, then weeks. We wrote letters, I ate like a king and slept peacefully for the first time in ages. And although we met no one who seemed to be the missing part of our crazy new family, we started looking. Every morning we'd get up and search for strange-looking kids. It was almost funny. Anyone with a tic, a limp, a dodgy stare or the slightest unusual way of doing *anything* caught our attention. But the twins appeared to have a nose for what they were expecting, and we never came across anyone who interested them at all. The following weeks I reckon we must have explored all of Coldharbour, and while we saw some weird sights ourselves, maybe we were the weirdest item traipsing about in Coldharbour that summer.

Then one day, after having been so caring of me, the twins' behavior changed.

For no reason they could explain, they started making me leave the shack. They were insistent about it, too, half-kicking me out during the day to go on aimless wanders. I could put up with that, but when they expected me to go out at night as well I had to say no. I wouldn't go out after dark, not in Coldharbour! The girls refused to leave me alone, though. Every evening they'd start up their heckling, trying to coax or shame me into a walkabout. After an hour or so they'd normally settle down and leave me in peace, but one evening they started up a great huffing and blowing and scratching. It went on without rest for several nights. I'd never heard such a racket! Then it got worse. They took to hissing in my ear—waiting until I fell asleep, then intentionally waking me up. Or, the next morning, they wouldn't get any food for breakfast. I was always hungriest in the morning—they knew that—but they'd just lounge around all day, deliberately irritating me.

I tried giving them a dab more of my beauty, but they didn't seem to need its comfort any longer. They wanted something else from it.

I didn't discover what that meant until a few days later.

The heat of that late summer! It never abated. All that sweat and noise and irritation in the confines of the shack! The full extent of my beauty revealed itself one sweltering night in September. It was a bad night, the worst so far that year: boiling, humid, merciless. The twins had started up about midnight, nipping my toes.

"Outside!" I demanded, when they wouldn't calm down. "Go on! Sleep outside! Get out. Now! I mean it!"

I nudged Emily with my foot. When she wouldn't move, I nudged a bit harder.

Suddenly she was excited, as if she wanted me to do it. That made me more nervous than anything she'd done before. "What's the matter with you?" I said. "Why are you acting so weird? I don't like it!"

"Poor Tommy," she pouted, glancing at Freda. "Don't like it, eh?"

"Ee's a sweaty man," Freda said. "Just shut up, will ee? Ah, poor Tommy, go to sleep. Little baby."

"You be quiet!" I said, trembling.

"If I'd a hand, I'd smack it," Emily said.

"If I'd a bone, I'd whack me with it!" Freda said.

"Whack you? What are you two on about?" I said. "What is the flipping matter with the both of you these days?"

They just laughed at me, and turned over to cuddle each other. Then Freda flicked my ear with her finger.

"I told you to get out of here!" I shouted.

"What'll yer do if we don't," she said, excited again, and sitting up. "What'll yer do, Tommy boy? What'll yer do?"

"I'll . . . I'll . . . "

I threw the sheets off and stumbled outside. My mind was in turmoil. What was happening? Why were the twins being so horrible? I couldn't stand it. Everything felt wild and scary to me that night. I didn't go back inside for ages. About an hour later the twins came out, said they were sorry and gave me a sort of cuddle, but I could tell they only half meant it.

The full extent of my beauty might have come out that night. If there had been anyone in Coldharbour who needed it, I think it would have done. But it waited until the next. A weather front came in, one of those freak summer cold snaps, and the night was chill.

A small girl was caught outside in it.

I don't know how much time she'd spent stumbling about before I found her. It might only have been hours; if you're badly dressed, it doesn't take long for a bitter night in Coldharbour to finish off your reserves of strength. Poor thing. She'd probably come in dressed for summer from one of the distant housing estates, maybe attached to a gang, and somehow got left behind. I found her on the far edge of the northeast dump, searching frantically for something to cover her arms.

Or, should I say, my beauty found her.

For it was my beauty itself that woke me. I sat up on my mattress with it simmering inside my mind. Without any hesitation I dressed in the dark. I could feel Emily and Freda next to me, silently excited.

"I'm going out," I said.

"Where to, Toms?" Freda asked.

"I don't know."

"Do you want uz to come wiv you?"

I thought about that. "Yes."

They put on coats, and scampered on either side of me as I strode into the night. I had several layers of clothing on, but I was still shivering soon after leaving the shack. The state of the girl we found was awful. You couldn't hear her. She was so cold she barely had a voice left. I would never have found her without my beauty. It led me, and as soon as it was close enough it acted.

From what depths, what part of me, did my beauty arise? I had no idea. All I knew was that its authority—its power—went in some way from me directly into her, into the frozen body of the girl. It was like a force, you could almost see it, a smack of warmth, something physical that entered her. It was a healing heat, yet at the same time it was an unbearable thrill that lit up every fiber of her, so intense that it frightened her.

Panting, she looked around—saw the twins on all fours—and started to run away.

"Don't go," I said. "It's all right. Emily and Freda won't harm you."

The twins withdrew into the darkness, sitting on their heels to avoid alarming her further. The girl was clearly still afraid of them, but she had no fear of me. I knew that because she walked up and leaned against my legs. She was no longer cold. As I picked her up, she put her cheek against my shoulder and began to cry.

Happy tears.

I placed my coat around her shoulders. The twins added items of their own, throwing the clothing from a distance. After compliments from Emily about how brave she'd been, the girl finally felt safe enough to let the twins approach. At first she wouldn't say a thing, but Emily, cracking jokes to make her laugh, soon got her address.

Then Freda crouched low, permitting the girl to take a ride on her back.

While the twins returned her to the town, I went back

to the shack. For an hour or so I just sat outside, staring at a few stars in the eastern sky. What had just occurred? My beauty was not the same hesitant force that had greeted the twins that first day on the dump. It was bolder now, a compression of so much luminous feeling that I was afraid.

I stayed out amongst the stars, waiting for Emily and Freda to return.

As soon as they did the girls were all over me with their affection. Both were laughing, happy, arms around each other, arms around me, ecstatic, unable to keep still.

"Before his beauty, the girl could only groan," Emily chanted.

"After his beauty, we took her 'ome," Freda said. She squeezed my arm, kissed my cheek sloppily and led me back into the shack. "It's all right, Toms," she said. "We went to her door, made sure she was found. And no one saw uz."

"What do you mean, all right?" I exploded. "How can anything be all right! What happened out there tonight? What happened?"

"It's really awake, Toms!" Emily whispered. "Your beauty—more than we ever needed! We knew there was!"

I closed my eyes. The twins were right. There was so much more beauty running though me than before. It was like a blaze, something I now sensed waited until it was needed by a specific child—and then acted. The girl tonight had only needed a dash of beauty, a droplet. It had far more to give. There's someone else coming, I realized. Not just a lost girl this time. Someone who needs *all* the beauty. I felt scared, trying to imagine the existence of anyone who could need so much.

The twins and I bedded down for the night. The girls quietened at once and lay alongside each other, but they were not asleep. They stared at me from the darkness in a sort of half-delighted, half-terrified awe.

"Are you okay, Tommy," Freda asked. "You wanna talk about it?"

"No, I want to think. We'll talk tomorrow."

"It's cold out there," Emily said. "Maybe there's more kids need help, eh?"

"No, there aren't," I said—and I knew it was true. Somehow my beauty knew that no one else in Coldharbour required its special services tonight.

"Let's try and get some rest now," I said.

Emily and Freda sighed, huddling close together. I propped my arms under my head and lay back on the sheets. I couldn't sleep, of course. At some point late in the night I recalled the face of the girl. Someone her age was bound to be in bed by now. I wondered if she was awake, still frightened by what had happened to her.

No sooner had I thought this than my beauty uncoiled and made itself ready. I hesitated, then sent it out to find the girl. She was a long way off, far beyond Coldharbour, but now that it knew of her existence my beauty found her easily. As I lay there, I extended it towards the girl, only softly, softly. I was trying something else; not the heat-surge I'd given her earlier; not a blast, something gentler. Could I control it? I needn't have worried. Now that her body had recovered, my beauty knew what the girl needed next. For a few moments it lingered in her mind, brushing her with tender thrills of reassurance, off and on, off and on. Then it left her alone to sleep peacefully. Later she dreamed—a nightmare—and my beauty woke me as it rushed back to her, and in her sleep the girl smiled.

I noticed the twins sitting up, watching me.

I cuddled up to them and we stayed like that, elated and awake the rest of the night.

the golden boy

MILO

Milo waited for the gang of boys to cross the river.

While he waited, he surveyed the night world of Cold-harbour. Everything was dark, but not to his new child-adapted eyes. He watched a boy's patch of light playing with a stray dog on one of the dumps. He looked beyond Coldharbour, and saw Jenny asleep in her bedroom. He saw the girl, Helen, lying on her right side, also sleeping.

He saw eight gang boys.

They had crossed the river, armed with clubs or other weapons, and were closing in.

Milo needed to get away, but his legs betrayed him. They had altered so much in the last hour that he had trouble walking. He could only make it a short distance from the river's edge before falling over. His feet felt clumsy. His knees could barely hold his weight.

For the first time Milo felt truly scared. I need my legs,

he thought. I need them to get away from the gang boys. Rubbing his thighs, he blundered as far from the river as he could. Then, realizing that he could never outrun the gang, he stopped and waited for them.

While he waited, he tried to focus on the extraordinary transformation of his body. Everything felt different. Even the weather, when it touched his skin, felt different. A wind arose, and Milo hunched into his sweater, but only out of habit. He wasn't cold at all. When he rubbed his fingers together they actually felt warm. I'll freeze out here tonight, he thought, seeing the clear skies overhead. I'm bound to freeze.

But he knew that wasn't true.

Minutes later, he heard the voices of the boys scrambling along the bank. He managed to stand up shakily to confront them. He could see the creamy light of the boys perfectly, but the gang were almost upon Milo before they saw him.

He decided to stay quiet. He would do or say nothing to provoke them.

"What is it?" one of the gang whispered, seeing his silhouette.

"I thought it was a kid," another said.

"That isn't a kid. It's . . . it's . . . *shining*."

All the boys stayed back, circling Milo, trying to make him out in the darkness. His silence unnerved them. "Who are you?" their leader yelled.

"It's coming from his arm," someone gasped. "Look at it!"

Milo glanced down. There was a small gash on his left wrist. He must have accidentally cut it while he was on the riverbank, though he could not remember doing so. There was no pain from the cut, but there was light spilling out—golden light.

Milo was intrigued rather than frightened. But he was frightened enough of the gang of boys. How could he defend himself? Thrusting his arm forward, he deliberately pulled the skin either side of the cut further apart. More gold splashed out, illuminating the ground. Milo widened the cut, feeling no discomfort.

All the boys staggered back.

"Let's get out of here," one said.

The gang leader picked up a stone and threw it, to prove that he wasn't afraid of Milo.

When the stone hit him, Milo pretended to feel nothing. He pulled the skin on his wrist back even further. There was no blood. He was able to peel the skin over his fingers, like a glove. He scratched his face—and one of the boys screamed. The entire gang backed away, some of them throwing sticks or other objects when they thought they were a safe distance.

Milo waited them out, and eventually the boys departed with curses and threats.

They'll come back, he knew. And next time there'll be more of them, better prepared. They won't be so afraid of me. They'll be expecting . . . a golden child.

My arm, he thought. For the next hour he stood there,

observing it from all angles. He felt its silkiness. He turned the gold in the darkness. On impulse, he rubbed his scalp—and a beam of soft yellow shot into the sky. The light would have been partially hidden if he still had hair, Milo realized. He wondered about that. He stared in awe at his body. It was hot. His old skin, when he pinched it, felt dead.

Then Milo felt the ground tremble under his feet, and he looked up.

Over a mile away a giant boy—twice the size of a man—was making his way into Coldharbour.

giant

THOMAS

A summer night. Moon and a sprinkling of stars. What more could you want?

Me and the twins were on a chase!

Emily and Freda led the way, sniffing the ground like they do, touching everything as they went along, loving it. Where were they going tonight? Some dead-end place again probably, with nothing to see when we got there. That's what had happened the last two evenings, but I followed them anyway. If they were on the trail of someone to add to our family, I was as anxious as them to find out who it would be.

Once Emily and Freda were underway, there was no stopping them. The twins: what grace of movement sometimes, running with an easy rocking motion on the callused balls of their hands and feet. There was no way I could keep up. They had to keep doubling back to urge me on.

Long before we arrived, I started feeling nervous. The twins were leading me to the western dump. By Coldharbour standards, this area represented rich pickings. Household items of considerable value like furniture were occasionally dumped here. It was the place the established gangs liked to congregate—well-organized kids, some of whom enjoyed making their own knives. Only an idiot messed with the gangs scrapping around this area, and I didn't like straying into their territory.

The twins didn't care about territories. As they entered the heart of the dump they became increasingly excited, heads sniffing the air, encouraging each other—and moving on. Luckily we didn't come across any of the gangs. What we came across was—well, what was it?

A boy, I suppose, but how could he be?

He was massive. I've seen big kids before and big men, men who trained to look the part and men who were just naturally strong. This boy belonged to some other order of strength. He was more like the foundations of a house than a boy. He was about twelve feet tall and five feet wide. His head was frightening, twice the size of a typical human head, the features in proportion but just too large—like a statue of a real head. His eyes were the length of my thumb. His neck was thick in the same way a horse's neck is thick.

The boy—if he was a boy at all—was hunched over the embers of a bonfire. He smiled, turning over the ashes. When he saw us we stopped: you bet we did! The twins huffed, making little eeking noises, wanting to go up to him—but even they were alarmed by a boy on this scale. What was he? Some kind of brute-man thing? No: I realized there was something much more eerie about him than that. It was his behavior. Usually the first sight of Emily and Freda freaked kids out, but this boy wasn't bothered by them at all. He just warmed himself in the remains of the bonfire, that strange smile on his face, rubbing his hands together. Those hands! Hands to grasp the world with! How could anything human be that size? He looked at us out of the corner of his eyes, but I don't think he was scared. Anything with his strength didn't need to be. There could have been ten of us with clubs, and I don't think he would have been concerned.

Was this the child my beauty was intended for?

I felt certain he must be. The boy didn't have any obvious needs, but surely a child of his sheer *size* was exactly what my beauty had been waiting for. Coming across him like this, I expected my beauty to rush out to fill whatever need he had. It didn't. It lay dormant. Emily glanced at me, clearly wondering the same thing, and I shook my head.

The giant boy dropped his left hand and picked up a section of scrap metal lying nearby. It was a car door. He casually lifted it into the air, not aggressively, just to show us that he could, I think—to show us what he could do.

I wanted to get away, but the twins showed no inclination to leave. This was their destination, I realized. They had brought me here to see this—this vastness of a boy. Where had he come from? I hadn't heard about him, and news travels fast in Coldharbour, especially about something like this. He must have just arrived.

Welcome to Coldharbour, I thought. If anyone can survive here, you can.

He was wearing an old blanket—actually several blankets—tied in odd ways around his body. He had no choice, I suppose; no manufactured clothes would fit him. Could he talk? He looked almost too big to be able to talk. It was frightening to think what nature of voice would emerge if he did.

I walked cautiously towards him, flanked by the twins. They had adopted a guarding role either side of me, and I was grateful. The boy let us approach. As we came closer he pivoted on his feet and turned to meet us. I felt the movement of his body through the ground, the weight of him.

He smiled. He held out his hand.

I wasn't sure what to do, but Emily and Freda didn't hesitate. They rushed over to him in the same way they had done to me the first time we met. Leaping over the ground Emily tickled his outsized feet, while Freda ran up his legs and pressed his big shoulders playfully. The boy grinned, then offered his hand again to me. That hand of his was too big to shake. I needed a bigger hand of my own to put inside it.

"Who—who are you?" I asked, keeping my distance.

The boy looked blankly at me. Then the muscles of his face slowly shifted. I could almost see the thoughts in his head cranking over.

How was I supposed to talk to him? I decided to try taking charge, show him that I wasn't afraid. It was a lesson I'd learned the hard way during my time alone in Coldharbour—if it's too risky to run, be as assertive as you dare.

"I asked you a question," I said loudly. "Are you dumb or something? Who are you?"

"What?" he said, in a voice that was surprisingly gentle. At last he seemed to understand me. "My name? Oh, my n-name, oh. My n-name is w-w-" He tried again. "My name is w-w-w-w-" He got stuck on that w for a while, and when I saw the embarrassment it caused him, I lost some of my fear. ". . . W-W-Walter," he said, giving me a great lopsided grin.

The twins smacked their hands gleefully and welcomed him at once.

"Where do you come from?" I demanded.

Walter glanced down at the remains of the fire as if the answer might be there. Maybe he came from a family of giants. A crazy image came into my head, then—of Walter, as a baby, with a normal-sized father taking his jeans off to find they fit his newborn. "You don't talk much, do you, Walter?" I said, determined not to soften my approach until I knew what we were up against. "I'm not exactly asking difficult questions here." The twins glared at me—they didn't like me goading him like this. "Come on," I insisted. "Where are you from?"

He finally mentioned a place so far away that I'd barely heard of it. "R-ran," he said. "R-ran." I realized he meant that he'd run all the way to Coldharbour from there. Looking at his legs, you could believe it.

"Why did you run?" I asked. He dropped his hands awkwardly, looking at me like I was the moon talking or something. "Try to think, Walter. What made you come here?"

Walter opened his mouth—and produced the roar.

We weren't ready for that. It was so unexpected that each of us screamed. We stopped when we saw the tears pouring down Walter's cheeks. He was shaking, as terrified as we were by the noise he had just made.

"S-sorry, s-s-sorry, should-should-shouldn't h-have," he said, holding out his arms to comfort us. "S-should n-never have . . . "

I looked at the twins, and saw they were thinking the same thing.

"Ee knows," Freda gasped. "Ee knows, Toms!"

"Take 'im wiv uz," Emily said. Then both twins went at it one after the other. "Please, Tommy! Take 'im 'ome! Take 'im wiv uz!"

Walter nodded wildly, clearly wanting to join us.

What was I going to do? The proportions of Walter, the fact that he knew about the roar, showed that in some way he was part of whatever was happening to us here.

But my beauty didn't recognize him. If he wasn't the one my beauty was waiting for, who was he? We had to be careful. Walter wasn't doing anything visibly threatening, but I was still too alarmed by his sheer size to bring him back to the shack. "You've got to be joking," I told the twins. "He can't stay with us. We can't take him to the shack! Look at him!"

"Ee's strong," Freda said.

"Ee can protect uz," Emily added.

"No," I said.

The twins squirmed.

"If I'd his fingers, they'd be too fat for rings," Emily said.

"If I'd his fingers, I'd grope and make fings," Freda said.

I studied Walter. Seeing him just there—just massively a presence there—I wondered if things bothered him in the same way as everyone else. Could he go weeks without eating? Did thirst or frost affect him? Dread: did he dread things like other boys?

Emily and Freda were right, in one regard. Walter was certainly strong. The twins were good guards, but we could all sleep easier, obviously, if we had this giant at our door. None of the gangs would come round to bother us then, ever—Walter would silence any neighborhood just by walking past it! But why should he help us? He hadn't exactly pledged his allegiance to me and the twins.

"I don't trust you," I told him. "Make me trust you."

Walter considered that. I got the impression that

making a case for his own merits wasn't something he'd been asked to do too often.

"Rain—I don't mind," he said. He frowned, then smiled as if the most brilliant thought in the world had just struck him. Regarding me with salesman-like shrewdness, he said, "I c-can live outside. I don't n-need anything."

I'll bet you don't, I thought.

"Rain—I don't mind," he said. "Snow—I d-don't mind. Hail, I—"

"Yeah," I said. "I get it. Hail—you don't mind." Bounces right off him probably, I thought. Or too scared to touch him.

The twins were nodding their heads vigorously, as if Walter's weather arguments were the most persuasive they had ever heard in their lives.

I stood there for a while, with the twins pleading with me. "No," I said at last. "Too risky."

I turned and started to walk away. The twins jumped with distress, but that was nothing compared with Walter's reaction. "I'm not b-bad!" he wailed. The power of his voice almost knocked me over, but I made myself carry on walking. With a single leap Walter jumped over my head and stood in front of me.

When I walked in another direction, I could see his lips trying to form new words, something more impressive. "I can b-build things," he said. "I can d-do things." As if to prove this, he butted the car door with his head. Then he took the edge of the door in one hand and with the other bent and twisted it until he had broken off a hunk of metal. He pummeled this into a bowl-like shape and held it out to me. When I didn't react, Walter licked his lips, glanced anxiously at the twins and tried again. He re-shaped the metal. With surprising delicateness he made another object. I couldn't believe it: the shape was a heart. A metal heart. With trembling hands, with reverence, he offered it to me.

"I don't want this," I said. "What am I supposed to do with it?"

Walter stared earnestly at me, and for a moment I thought he was going to cry. The twins were looking at me as though I was a bit of scum. They clearly weren't frightened of Walter, but that only made me more hesitant; maybe this was one occasion I needed to remain alert and watchful for all three of us.

"There's no room in the shack for him," I told the girls.

"Yes, there is," Freda said—and, of course, she was right. A shiver ran through me, thinking about that. "We can't trust him," I said. "He won't do what he's told."

"I will," Walter said.

I shook my head, but his face was so amiable that it was hard to mean it.

"If I bring you back to where we live," I said, "what are you going to do there?"

Walter glanced at the twins, obviously seeking advice.

"Anything ee says," Freda whispered to him. "Tell 'im that."

Walter nodded. He smiled at me. "Anything you says!"

I grinned—it was a good imitation of Freda—but I stood there a little longer, unable to decide. Walter's smile never faded. Eventually I picked up his metal heart and said, "Do you want to come with us then, or are we going to just stand around here all flipping night?"

And do you know what Walter did? A grin twice as wide as any you've ever seen lit up his whole face. His humongous brown eyes sparkled with happiness, and he came over and kissed me. Not on the face, but the hand. It felt like having a vacuum cleaner on my skin, trying to scoop up my palm, but it was obvious how genuinely he meant it.

And do you know what: I laughed. I couldn't help it. I'd had all this fear of him, and suddenly I knew that whatever else I needed to know about Walter, I didn't have any need to fear him.

"You won't like it," I said, trying to explain to Walter about the life of Coldharbour. But he wasn't even listening, was he? He just kept looking at me and the twins in awe, as if we'd given him an everlasting pass to every theme park in the world.

We set off home. I shook my head, hardly able to believe that I was taking him back to the shack. The twins whooped with joy. Freda tracked ahead of us, while Emily remained with Walter, bringing up the rear. Walter stayed behind me the whole way, taking tiny slow steps to avoid overtaking me.

"Stay quiet," I told him. "It's dangerous round here. We don't want anyone seeing you." I don't know why I bothered to say that. Half the night gangs in the neighborhood were watching us. Anyway, the twins were making a right old din, as usual.

Even so, Walter tried to keep quiet. He put the slab of one of his fingers to his lips, as if that would do the trick. But he couldn't keep it up for long. The twins kept running up to him, shrieking and tickling him, and on top of that you could see how excited and pleased he was. I sent a snippet of beauty out to Walter, only a taste, and his eyes just filled up with the biggest joyful tears you ever saw. Seeing this, the twins were running all around him at once, yammering on. Over and over they reassured Walter, singing their dippy rhymes, and checking with him every few yards to make sure that he was okay.

For a while Walter maintained his discipline. He kept glancing at me, putting his hand full over his lips to prevent himself making a sound. But at some point he forgot and started joining in with the twins' banter, trying to copy one of their rhymes in his stuttery way.

"If I'd a bone, I'd bite it!" screeched Emily.

"If I'd a smile, I'd light it!" Freda wailed.

"If-if-if—" Walter went. "If-if—"

And then we were all laughing and falling about, weren't we, with the gangs looking on in disbelief at the four of us, and Walter rocking the earth as he clumped along, dragging the remains of the car door, booming out his stutters, measuring out one titchy step to every three strides of mine, and all of us making enough racket to wake the dead.

s k i n

MILO

Milo knew he had to find a place to hide before the gang boys returned.

Sufficient cloud that night drifted across the sky to cover the moon, but his own golden arm glowed like a moon itself. Where could he go? He packed the shining parts of him in mud from the river's edge, smearing his skin until it was dark. Then, with great difficulty, he managed to shuffle away from the river.

There was an abandoned brickyard not far away. He hid under the rubbish in a large industrial bin. The gang kids, in reinforced numbers, came back to search the area, but did not find him.

Relieved, Milo removed the mud from his body and stroked the gleaming area. There was a clear dividing line at his elbow between his different skins. His old skin felt heavy, ancient, wrong. He placed the nail of a thumb on his bicep muscle, finding that he could pull the skin apart easily here—but the skin still resisted further up, nearer the shoulder.

He left it, uncertain what to do next. For a time, he slept.

Around midnight the skin on the shoulder of his golden arm clicked, splitting open. A few hours later Milo woke up, climbed out of the bin and started taking off the rest of his skin.

He stood there, entirely golden, lighting up the brickyard.

What am I? he thought, trembling. What kind of thing?

Just a boy, he tried to convince himself. Still a boy.

It was when he started to climb back into the bin that he heard the sound of the roar for the first time. Initially he thought it was merely a trick of the wind, or perhaps the grunt of an unusual animal heard between the gusts. He listened more closely, and realized that the sound was more like a shriek. He forgot about everything else. For hours he turned and turned his head, listening to the cold depths of the roar. Only when the fullness of night arrived did the sound of it gradually fade into the background.

Milo stood there, breathing deeply, feeling more frightened than he ever had in his life.

What creature is making that noise? he wondered. What heartless thing?

He slept uneasily for the remainder of the night.

In the morning he hid behind some girders and watched the gangs. His improved eyes could tell exactly what each child was doing. One tough-looking teenager, thinking no one could see him, was bending to sniff a flower on the western dump. Milo smiled, and once again felt an unaccountable urge to climb to the highest point in Coldharbour's flat landscape, and from there call out to all the gangs.

Sighing, he moved round the brickyard. For some reason he enjoyed being here. He wandered around it, touching every chunk of concrete and piece of steel the builders had left behind. Then, covering himself up, he walked out of the brickyard and explored the nearest Coldharbour dump. He liked the shape of it. He liked the untidiness of it. Even the cold soil under his feet felt good. He looked up, enjoying the sight of each scrap of rubbish blowing to and fro on breezes coming in off the sea.

Somehow I belong in this place, he thought. I don't want to leave it.

He returned to the bin, with no idea what would happen next. All he understood was that the changes inside his body felt natural, and were still only the beginning.

Dawn arrived, and birds pecked at him through the rubbish. Feeling hungry, Milo wrapped himself in torn plastic sheeting and anything else he could find and scoured the dumps for food. His new stomach was tougher than the old one, and that was just as well because his appetite now seemed to be virtually endless. He ate continuously, for hours, without putting on a sliver of extra weight. And after eating he drank: straight from the river, an enormous amount.

Returning to the brickyard, Milo dozed again. When he woke, for several minutes he simply lay amongst the rubbish in the bin, glistening like a small sun inside. His skin was now all golden, but there was a second color. If he scratched hard enough at his wrist, he discovered silver. It was only a tiny amount, a crack, but it shone so radiantly that he could hardly bear to look at it.

Gold is not my final color, he realized.

Yet it hurt to scratch down deeper, and at last Milo understood something: his eyes, his golden skin, his failing legs, were only small changes. The ones to come next would be so huge that they were going to be painful. I'm going to be ill, he realized. I won't be able to get through this on my own. I'm going to need other people.

In that moment Milo wanted his mother. But he also knew that no ordinary person—not even his mother with all her love—could help him prepare for what was next. He tried to shout out loud, but he could not even do that. It was now agony even to talk. He clutched at his throat, sensing how much it had altered in the last few hours. Did nothing in his old body work as it should? He felt suddenly furious. To be able to eat so much, but not to speak! To be capable of drinking vast quantities from the river, but not be able simply to walk, to put one foot in front of the other . . .

Milo clutched at his stomach, an ache tugging at him.

What now? he thought. Hauling himself to the top of the bin, he looked out.

Come on, he ordered his eyes; find someone for me.

They cooperated at once, zoning in on a shack in the northern part of Coldharbour. Focusing on it, they frantically plotted the fastest path to get there. Now—with the final transformations about to beset him—Milo at last knew how desperately he needed to reach one particular boy inside that shack. Was it too late?

His eyes screamed at his legs to move.

Milo hauled himself to the top of the bin. He pushed his dead feet over the sides and lowered his weight down. But before he dropped to the ground he gazed one more time in the direction of a farmhouse outside Coldharbour. The girl, Helen, was that way. His eyes sought her out, tracing her distinctive patch of light from an upstairs bedroom, across a hallway. He followed her as she opened her front door, traveling along a path fringed with forget-me-nots.

There she was, walking.

Milo gripped the metal edges of the bin and watched her. He even called out to her.

To Helen, Milo reached out with all his heart.

EIGHT

the astounding call

HELEN

I fell onto the forget-me-nots by the path.

"Who's there?" I demanded, staring wildly in all directions. Surely someone had called out my name? But the fields were empty, the path clear, with home too far for any shout from Dad to have reached me.

And then I heard it again, calling out more urgently.

It was an astounding call, a voice of wonder.

For several minutes I crouched tensely on the path, my heart hammering. I couldn't think. I only knew that I wanted to hear that voice again. I waited, but the call faded on the wind. Finally I picked myself up, stumbling dazedly around in my sneakers. Where I'd struck the ground there was a bruise on my cheek. I didn't notice. I forgot the original reason I'd had for being on the path and started searching.

Without knowing why, I listened for anything out of the ordinary. I felt in dark places under hedgerows. I pushed through brambles, ignoring the cuts to my hands. I checked the hollows of trees, as if an incredible face might be inside them. Once I found myself staring out over Coldharbour, and wondered why I had turned that way.

I was looking for—for what exactly? Something I had never known before. Something extraordinary: an angel in a field; a child aflame; I don't know what.

A boy. Suddenly I knew it was a boy, and I felt like weeping. A boy, slightly younger than me, had made those wonder-filled calls.

But how could that be true? How could it be?

I don't know how many hours passed before I staggered home. On the way back I felt odd. I felt . . . *surrounded.* I paused, looking in all directions. There was no one nearby—I was alone on a track between two fields. Even so, I sensed countless eyes on me. Insects, I realized with shock. They were everywhere: gripping the path, up in the air, crawling under the soil.

What was happening?

Perched on a nearby leaf, a ladybird held its wings open. It's warming them, I thought. It's not ready to fly yet. It's too cold. It's warming them first in the sun.

How could I possibly know that?

I continued walking home, acutely aware of every bug on the path. I tried not to step on them. Other creatures were studying me from the safety of bushes and trees: birds. I couldn't see them, but I felt their presence, furtively watching.

I stopped. A snail clung to the underside of a large boulder. I knew where to find it, a few feet off the path. I walked over, lifted the boulder—and the snail shrank away from the light.

I ran the rest of the way home.

Dad was there, standing at the garden gate. "Helen!" he said. "It's been hours! Where —" Seeing the mud on my face, he hurried down the path. "What is it? Are you hurt? Let me look at you."

I wasn't ready to tell Dad, not yet. I needed some time to think first.

"It's nothing," I murmured. "I . . . I fell over, that's all."

"Fell over? Did you hit your head? Were you unconscious, even briefly?"

"No, it . . . wasn't that bad."

Dad examined my face, satisfying himself that the injury was minor. "Helen, I was worried sick!" he said. "Where on earth have you been all this time?"

"I got . . . lost."

"Lost? Around *here*?" He clearly wanted to ask further questions, but something about my expression stopped him. "Okay," he said. "Come on." He led me inside, and I realized that he was removing my coat and shoes. I sat on the couch, feeling unreal. Dad sat beside me.

"Helen, what's going on?"

"Nothing. I—"

"Nothing? Come off it. You're trembling! What happened out there?"

I don't know, I thought. I don't know! I wanted to tell him, but I needed to make sense of it myself first. Behind the sofa a spider nestled, distracting me. I could sense its hunger.

"Dad, I . . . I'll tell you, but I need to rest for a bit first. Just a nap, that's all." I glanced up, silently imploring him to ask nothing more.

"Helen, if—"

"Dad, please."

He studied me closely. "Okay," he said, letting out a deep breath. "If that's what you need. A nap. All right, Helen." He was riddled with anxiety, but instead of asking anything more he just kissed me nervously on the forehead and followed me upstairs.

I traipsed off to the bathroom and cleaned myself up. Then, offering Dad a weak smile, I went to my bedroom. I closed the door. For a while I just lay on the bed, staring at the ceiling. The boy: I wondered about him, thrilled by him, scared of him. I wanted to hear his astounding wonder-calls again. I got up and wandered across to the window. For the second time that day I found myself staring out over Coldharbour.

Did the mysterious boy live in that place? Was he there alone?

Without undressing, I pulled aside the sheets and slipped inside. I tried to relax. I couldn't, of course—there was too much to stimulate me. Like insects skittering and sliding round the house. They were in every room, and the garden was thick with them: dozens of grim battles of survival taking place in the sunshine. And this, I realized, wasn't the first time I'd felt their small fears. For weeks similar intrusive half-thoughts and blurry feelings had been filtering through to me. But those had only come when I was alone or at night, and I'd barely been aware of them. What I was experiencing now was entirely differ-ent. Every oozing fear in the garden was open to me, every peck of death.

Merciless nature, I thought. What have I become part of?

For over an hour I lay on my bed, listening in on the noises of this creature-filled world. And the longer I lis-tened, the more I became aware of a particular noise. The sound of it carried to me like a howl. I listened closely, and it was more like a roar. I lay there, increasingly dis-turbed by it until I heard a hesitant shuffle outside my room.

"Helen, are you asleep?"

"No. Come in, Dad."

He'd brought a hot drink. After handing it to me he walked slowly across to the window and stared out into the garden.

"I'm okay," I said. "I'm fine . . . " I forced a smile.

"Fine? If that's true, why is your hand shaking?" He walked over and sat next to me on the bed, taking the cup out of my hand. "And what are these tear-stains all about? More evidence of how fine you are?"

I lowered my eyes.

"Tell me," he said. "Helen, it doesn't matter what happened. If you're in trouble, if it's something you've done, I'm not going to get angry with you, no matter what it is."

"No, it's . . . come on." Trembling, I got out of bed, took his hand, led him downstairs. There was a beetle under the fridge. I forced Dad to get down on his knees to see it there. Then I took him into the garden. "Ants," I said, parting the grass to show him. "Toiling away. They never stop."

"Helen, I don't understand—"

"You will."

I tugged him back to the kitchen. "A fly," I said. "It's trapped. They get trapped all the time. They don't understand how things work!" I indicated the bluebottle buzzing under the net curtain. I opened the window and, half-laughing, half in disbelief, felt the alarm ebb out of that tiny creature.

Dad stared at me. "Helen . . . how do you know these things?"

And then I felt something else, something new and much more harrowing. It was Dad, in shock. It was his thoughts, his frantic concern for me.

"You . . . " I stepped back—almost screamed.

I was in Dad's mind, and to be inside there was so much more frightening than the creatures in the garden or house. Dad was terrified. He was trying to formulate any sort of question that would make sense. Or was I mistaken?

"Think of a number," I said. "I have to be sure."

"What? Helen, I don't . . . "

"Just do it, Dad. Don't say what it is . . . fifty-nine," I told him, as soon as he formed the thought. I reeled off several others in succession.

"You're reading my mind!"

I nodded, shaking with fear, trying to hold myself together. Dad led me into the living room, and we parked ourselves side by side, staring at each other. Dad was silent, but I was overwhelmed by all the details of his concern for me.

"When —"

" . . . Did it start? Just now. Just now!" I hesitated. "No, wait, that's not true."

I told him about the feelings I'd had the last few weeks, and about the boy. Dad didn't want to believe it. He preferred to believe that I'd had some kind of minor breakdown, something normal he could understand and deal with. But as I read his thoughts back to him, Dad had no choice other than to believe.

"This boy," he said at last. "Do—"

"No, I don't know him. I don't know anything about him."

"Do you think—let me finish, Helen," he said, as I started to interrupt. "Do you think he's trying to harm you?"

"Harm me? No, of course not." I said it automatically, then sat back to think. That the boy might be dangerous had never occurred to me.

"Consider what actually happened," Dad said. "You fell down, hit your head, not badly, but it could have been worse. The boy seems to have been the cause. Did he do it deliberately?"

"No," I replied, certain now. "When I fell, bruised myself, that was just an accident. I was shaken by his voice, that's all. He wasn't trying to hurt me. He . . . "

"Go on."

"He's in some kind of trouble, Dad."

"I thought you said the boy didn't speak at all, except to call out your name."

"He didn't."

"So why do you think he's in trouble?"

"I don't know. But he needs . . . help."

Dad held my hand. "What's wrong with him, Helen?"

"I don't know."

"Do you have any idea where he is?"

"No."

Don't do anything stupid. I don't want to lose you.

Wham! It was a thought that came out of nowhere, flashed out of Dad. He was looking right at me, and in his mind I looked different, beautiful. I realized then that's how he always saw me. To Dad my face was beautiful in a way that was entirely related to his feelings for me.

"Oh Dad," I said, burying my face in his shoulder.

"What is it?" he asked. But I think he knew, and then all sorts of emotions were pouring out of him, weren't they. Unbidden ones. Of Mum. She died after an illness when I was only a few months old, but suddenly, right there, Dad brought her vividly to life. She was there. And the way I was seeing her was not as a daughter, but the way only Dad knew her. I saw what she looked like in the morning, as she turned towards him.

Dad glanced away from me, but I wasn't embarrassed.

"I want to know more," I said huskily.

"Later . . . " Dad whispered. "I'm not ready for this yet, Helen. I'm not sure you are either."

I nodded, but all I wanted at that moment was Mum back; I wanted to be lost in his mind with her forever.

Dad left me to recover in the living room while he went to the kitchen to make us something to eat. By the time he returned, he had collected his thoughts. "Whatever this gift of yours means, it's clearly linked to the boy," he said. "We need to decide what we're going to do if you hear him again, or if he decides to pay us a visit in person. Helen, are you positive you can't tell me anything more about him?"

"He's ill," I said, with absolute certainty. "He's . . . " I burst into tears, without knowing why. "He's . . . *burning*."

"Burning?" Dad said hoarsely. "What do you mean?"

I stared at him, with no idea what had made me use such a word.

Dad formulated a plan for the rest of the day. Every door and window locked. No going outside. No separation at any time. I could have privacy in my room, but only if he was in the next one. If the boy made any further mental contact with me, we would decide together what to do. No sleeping unless Dad was awake. I was not to answer the door. I would do nothing without consulting him first.

At some point in the afternoon, after Dad had satisfied himself that the house was secure, he said, "Helen, I've never seen you looking so tired. Why don't you have a nap for a couple of hours? Actually, I'll bring a chair into your bedroom, stay there with you a while . . . "

"I'll be all right," I said, wanting Dad close but feeling the need to be alone as well. "I'll find it hard to sleep if you're next to me."

In the end he reluctantly agreed, but only after wedging my door open and preparing the adjoining guest bedroom for himself. "Don't close your door for any reason," he said, "and shout if you need anything. I won't be asleep." He kissed me, started to leave. At the door he stopped. "Can you really tell *everything* that's going on in my head?"

"Yes, I think so."

"I suppose I'll have to find a way to keep only the finest of thoughts in there at all times, then." He grinned. "I'll never manage it, though."

"Don't worry," I said. "I won't peep."

But I did, of course. With Dad so close I didn't have any choice. I tried to tune out of his mind, but with all the emotions scattering out of him it was impossible. Dad was close to tears. He was sitting in an armchair, thinking about me—and then his thoughts switched to Mum, to their last days together. He missed her so much that suddenly I could hardly bear to be in his mind any longer. And then I just buried my head in the pillow, keeping the crying sounds down so that he wouldn't have to hear them.

A gift, Dad had called it. I wasn't convinced about that. What kind of a gift makes you cry? I hated the endless creature deaths in the garden, but they weren't my main concern. I'm going to be afraid of people, I realized. I'm not going to want all their thoughts. Dad—sometimes I'm going to be afraid of you, too. I already am.

Eventually I managed to fall asleep.

In my dreams I saw a boy burning in a bin.

NINE

treasures

THOMAS

I liked Walter right away, but I wasn't taking any chances.

I decided to test him by leaving him outside the shack that first night—not for long, just to see what he would do. I half-expected him to slink off; either that or we'd hear those generous-sized knuckles of his banging against the door to be allowed inside for company.

The rain started about midnight, only a shower. "Rain—I don't mind," he'd said. The twins went crazy at me to let Walter in, but I resisted. About half an hour later, I checked on him.

And there he was, holding the car door over his head, smiling back as if he loved it out there.

"You all right, Walts?" Freda asked worriedly. "You wanna come in?"

Walter gave her his best lopsided grin.

"Nah, n-n-n-nice out h-here," he said, fanning himself with the door.

I tried to get some sleep after that, but it was hard with Walter's immense shape plonked out there—especially when he started humming quietly to himself. The rain gradually worsened, driven by a stiff breeze. Between gusts I could hear Walter whistling. The twins, of course, were livid about me leaving him outside, and finally I relented. I wanted to be tough on Walter until I was sure we could trust him, but not that hard.

So I opened the door, intending to let him in.

And there he still was, in exactly the same spot, car door over his head, smiling away.

But there was a change. We use a corrugated section of plastic as a windbreak outside the shack. Sometime in the past hour Walter had repositioned this, altered the angle so that it shielded us better. He had also firmed up the shack's foundation supports, making certain they were safely sunk into the wet ground.

Walter himself was soaked through.

"If I'd a kindness, I'd bring 'im in," Freda said.

"If I'd a heart, I'd give it 'im," Emily said.

I looked at the long sandy hair plastered all over Walter's face, and suddenly felt ashamed of myself. "Come on," I said, smiling at him. "I think the twins have got some blankets all ready."

Walter shook his head, no.

"It's all right," I said. "I don't know how, but we'll squeeze you in somewhere."

Walter shook his head again—solemnly, still holding

the car door up, as if it represented perfect all-weather protection. This was too much for the twins. They raced out, trying to yank him towards the shack. Of course, you couldn't yank Walter anywhere. He simply wouldn't budge.

"Look, just come in," I said. "We're *all* getting wet now!"

"N-no," Walter said. "I l-like it!"

"What? You like it outside?"

He nodded fervently, trying to cover Emily and Freda with the car door, obviously concerned that they were getting wet. "G-go in! In!" he urged. He hulked over them, using his back to keep the rain off their bodies.

The twins were as confused as me. Finally, with a strangled cry, Walter picked both girls up—one in each hand—and carried them back to the shack. Then, filling his cheeks, he blew a warm, drying air stream over them. They wriggled with pleasure, giggling and tossing their hair—but still trying to get Walter to come into the shack.

Walter refused. He plopped himself down in his old position in the mud, with the car roof stubbornly back over his head.

"This is flipping ridiculous!" I shouted.

"N-not s-safe," he said.

"What do you mean, not safe? Of course it's safe!" Was he worried for himself? "We'll look after you!"

"Not s-safe." Walter sat there doggedly repeating this,

as if it was obvious what he meant. Then, in frustration, he yelled, "Look who's c-coming!" His eyes darted about as if thousands of enemies were attacking at once. "See!" he exclaimed. When we didn't he crammed himself within the shack and said, "They're c-coming! Can-can't see!"

Suddenly, it clicked. He couldn't see danger approaching from inside the shack.

"You can protect us better, easier, from out here?" I said. "Is that it?"

He grinned his lopsided best.

"Don't be stupid," I said. I ran out and this time we all tried shoving him inside. Walter wasn't having any of it. He—very gently—removed us from his body, placed us in the shack, and went back to his place in the rain.

For a while the twins and I just watched him from the doorway.

Eventually—when all reasoning with him failed—we went back to bed. Between gusts of wind I could hear Walter whistling again. The twins glanced over at me.

"Ee's here to protect uz," Freda murmured. "Ee don't know why, but it's all ee talked about on the way here." Then she added, "We're a proper family now, ain't we? A beauty boy, two insect-girls and a giant."

I stared at her nervously. "Is this all of us, then? The entire family?"

Both girls seemed uncertain. "If there's any more," Freda said, "we'll go and find 'em."

"And Walts, kind dear," Emily added, "will care and mind 'em."

Both girls soon fell into a contented sleep, but I couldn't settle at all that night. A giant, I thought. A giant to protect us. What monstrous creature was coming that required a child of Walter's strength to lie in wait for it?

Finally the rain let up, and I heard the car door being placed delicately down—Walter making sure he didn't wake us. All night he stayed out there, his breathing deep over the wind.

By the time I woke next morning Walter had nearly dried out, with only a few wisps of steam still wending from his blankets. Some of the local gang kids were staring at him as if he was something terrifying that had grown in the night. They kept their distance.

A good start, I thought, to Walter's new career.

The twins were already up, telling Walter about the area where we lived. "There's boys, they're no good, out west-aways," Freda was saying. "Sometimes, Walts, they come at night, and nicks stuff, try anyways, or just makes a racket, and . . ."

Walter nodded thoughtfully. From time to time he asked Freda to pause, making her say things over and over again until he completely understood. She took his heavy hand, swinging it to show him the directions the gang kids came from. "How m-m-many kids?" I heard him ask.

"Lor' knows, Walts," Freda said, more interested in sniffing his musty brown blankets. "You can't wear these," she told him. "You need some proper clothes." She picked at a sodden bit of blanket dangling over his foot. "We'll make yer some."

"I'm f-fine," he said, surveying the horizon through narrowed eyes. "The gang kids, they g-g-got weapons, eh?"

"Ooh, everything, Walts. Knives, sticks. If I'd a gun, I'd pack a punch."

"If I'd a gun, I'd eat your lunch!" Emily said.

The twins rolled about on the ground, but Walter just gave a long grave nod, peering suspiciously about him.

God almighty, I thought, what's going on in his head?

Actually, we knew a little about Walter now. The twins had been up with him since dawn, and apparently he'd started growing into a giant only weeks ago—the same time, in fact, that I'd left home, and the twins had dropped on all fours and made their first scuttles across a carpet.

"But me and Emms," Freda explained, "at least 'ad each other, Toms, didn't we? Kids screamed and ran, but there was two of uz when we needed comforting. Walter—ee don't seem to have had no one, just a Dad ee can't remember who left when ee was just a baby, and a mum ee ran away from when ee changed, she was so afraid of 'im. Emms reckons ee's just been staying out of sight ever since, until something brought him here.

Brought him to uz. Let's be good to 'im, Toms," she said softly. "Let's do things for 'im."

"Like what?" I asked. "You heard what he said—he doesn't need anything."

Freda gave me a scathing glance. "Ee just said that to get you to listen to 'im last night!" She sized Walter up with her eyes. "C'mon," she said, prodding Emily in the belly. "We both know what ee needs!"

With a conspiratorial giggle the twins went running off.

I stayed behind, wondering about Walter. I looked at him and really wondered what I'd got myself into. He clearly wanted to protect us, but how effective would he be? There seemed to be no real malice in him. He was almost too affectionate. The first time anyone saw his shadow they'd be terrified, but once they spotted that lopsided grin . . .

However, Walter surprised me. He was eager to learn. He wanted to know all about Coldharbour—the geography, the dangerous areas, the most threatening gangs. We also worked together on some routines for safeguarding the shack—protection drills, I called them. Walter really took to this, and we went at them all morning. By lunchtime I'd had enough, but Walter wanted to carry on.

"So what are you going to do if this place is attacked?" I asked him for about the fiftieth time.

"Protect you!"

"Yeah? How you gonna do that, then?"

"Any w-w-way I can!"

"Show me!"

He looked at me sneakily. "Depends," he said, remembering what I'd told him.

"Depends on what?"

"Depends on w-w-what the d-danger is, Tommy!" He grinned, imitating my voice. "No p-p-point running a-about l-like a t-twit not being sure what the h-h-heck you're doing, right?"

"Right," I said, trying to keep a straight face. "Okay, what if one of the gang kids comes round, trying to steal things?"

Walter sprinted around the shack, making an almighty scare-off noise like King Kong himself about to tear the place apart. "Build a trench!" I said. Within seconds, Walter's hands were plunged into the earth, creating a groove all around the shack large enough to hold me inside. Walter placed me there, jumped in himself and crouched down, with only his eyes and forehead showing over the top. "They've breached the trench!" I shouted. "The scrappers are in the shack! They're after us! What do you do now?" Fire burned in Walter's eye: righteous anger. He picked me up and drew me to his chest; his other arm pointed outward like a shield.

"Put me down," I said—and he did, though he took his time. Walter had a habit of doing this sometimes, getting carried away.

I stood beside him, looking out over Coldharbour. A few of the gangs were watching us, but I couldn't hear their conversations. It wasn't the wind drowning them out. It was something much more menacing than that: the roar. The sound of it was much louder now.

"I don't think these protection drills are going to be much use against whatever's making that sound," I said.

Walter nodded his head dolefully. Then he opened his mouth.

"Don't," I cried, thinking he was going to imitate the roar again.

"N-no," he said. He held me gently, stroking my face. "I won-won't s-scare you again, Tommy. I w-won't l-let anything h-hurt y-you. Listen." He took a deep breath; then, holding onto it, dragged his arms backwards and forwards through the air.

I almost laughed. "What are you up to?"

Walter kept going, and gradually his heavy arms produced a whooshing noise. I recognized it. Since yesterday the twins and I had been hearing it, too.

It was a slow rhythm, like a massive wing beating against the sky.

"What is it?" I marveled. "Do you know?"

Walter shook his head, but his gigantic eyes lit up. "N-not the roar," he said. "I th-think . . . Tommy . . . it's something . . . b-better."

"An enemy," I whispered. "An enemy of the roar."

As soon as I said it, I could see that Walter felt the same way. He continued to flap his arms. For a while he even managed to block out the sound of the roar altogether, and for a moment I had some peace at last from that endless cold shrieking. And I thought: perhaps there'll be a weapon, after all. If anything can make a stand against the roar, I thought, it beats with the power of those wings.

In the early afternoon the twins returned from a visit to the tips. They were carrying scraps of cotton, linen, denim, needles, thread and who knows what else. "Hey!" I protested, as they grabbed Walter and hustled him inside the shack.

"You shuts your moanin', Walts," I heard Freda say firmly, closing the door. "You'll get back out there when you got some decent stuff on yer. Now stay still!" I waited outside, listening. Walter protested as they measured him up. He kept telling them to hurry up, that he didn't need a hat. At one point it became suddenly silent. Then I heard Emily say, "Walts, you're gonna 'ave to let that blanket go if we're gonna fit these pants on yer."

About an hour later the door reopened. There was a moment of hesitation. Then Walter emerged. I tried, not very hard, to keep a sober expression on my face. Walter staggered out, feeling his new clothes.

"H-how do I look?" he asked.

"You look good," I said. "Real good."

His trousers were made from about a hundred separate

bits of blue denim sewn roughly together. They had flares at the bottom, with little flowers around the hems—obviously from a girl's old pair. For a shirt the twins had patched together a woolly brown jumper and a black leather jacket. I think there was a scarf sewn in there somewhere, too. The jacket only stretched down to Walter's elbows, and Freda was hanging onto him like a monkey, trying to pull the sleeve further down with both her arms. No shoes, of course—even the twins couldn't manage that. Walter's feet stuck out like boats.

"I've got a p-pocket," he told me, tapping at the left side of his chest. There was some kind of school badge there, with an opening underneath. The pocket was too small for Walter to get his fingers inside.

The twins exchanged anxious glances.

"Well, o' course it needs improvement," Freda said contemplatively. "Not much light in the shack to see wiv, you know."

"Yeah, we'll make it better, definitely," Emily added. "Just takes time."

"Them underpants not too uncomfortable, Walts?" Freda asked.

"They're f-f-f-f-fine," he replied—with real dignity, I thought.

After a late-afternoon snack and a few improvements from the twins on the trousers, Walter and I put on a bit of a show for the girls—a couple of defensive maneuvers.

"G-g-got a surprise!" Walter said, when we were finished.

"Oh yeah," I replied. "What's that then?"

"You s-sneak up," Walter said. "You go off, away from the s-shack. Close y-your eyes."

Nonplussed, I did as he asked. A minute later the twins called me back. Walter was nowhere in sight. The twins shrugged extravagantly, as if they had absolutely no idea where he'd gone.

"Sneaks up," Freda said.

So I did. Where was Walter? How could he just disappear? When I was only a few feet from the shack, the earth erupted. I was flung into the air. As I fell the hand of Walter caught me. He had dug himself into the ground, and now my waist lay squeezed between the fingers of one of his hands.

The twins raced between his legs, laughing away.

"If I'd an arm, I'd chuck it!" Freda squealed.

"Go on, Walts! Go on, Walts!" Emily encouraged him.

Walter pulled back his arm like a slingshot.

I said something like, "AAAAGGGHHHHH!"

"No!" screamed the twins. "Walts! Not really! Not really!"

Walter gave me and the twins his best confused look. Then his eyes twinkled mischievously. "Ha ha ha ha!" he boomed. He let go of me and put me down as sweetly as a baby. I stumbled around for a minute, trying to recover.

One of the twins whispered gleefully, "Tommy, 'ope

yer didn't wet yer pants."

I checked—just in case.

That evening I worked out a little return joke to play on our Walter—just a bit of playfulness. When I told the twins, they were game for it.

"One more protection situation," I said, striding out of the shack. Walter was up and ready at once. "The twins have been taken!" I hollered. "Red alert! Red alert! You weren't here! You didn't get here in time! They're gone!" Walter shook his head emphatically. I laughed. "You screwed up!" I yelled. "They're hurt. You failed!" No, no, Walter kept shaking his head, and opening out his arms at the twins, as if to say, "What? You're all here. I have protected you."

"You haven't protected us!" I shouted. "The twins are dead. Look!" At my signal the girls feigned death. Dropping to the ground, they closed their eyes.

Walter exploded! He ran up to them, shrieking. He touched their faces, picking them up, in tears. I started laughing and so did the twins, both sitting up again. Suddenly Walter realized that it was a joke. For a moment he didn't laugh, but then, hesitantly, he started chuckling— that big grin of his stretched across his face.

But not really. He didn't smile for long. He wasn't really chuckling at all. As soon as we stopped, so did he. Then Walter sighed, a shudder of concern that racked his whole body. Shaking his head, he carried the twins reverentially over to me and put us into a neat pile. I laughed again, slightly embarrassed, but Walter just put his arms around the three of us and held us closely for a while. We looked up at him, and suddenly we felt humble. You could see it in his face: if anything bad happened to us, anything at all, it would just kill him.

"We're all right," I said hoarsely. "Walter—you can let go."

Who was this extraordinary boy? Only yesterday I'd rejected him, left him out in the rain, ordered him about, called him dumb, yet here he was holding us, with big tears brimming in his eyes, cradling and rocking us as if we were treasures.

TEN

the long inconsolable cry

HELEN

I woke that night to the sound of the boy again.

But not the wonder-filled calls this time. Those had been replaced by a long inconsolable cry, like blood across the night. I leapt out of bed, tearing aside the curtains as if *he* might actually be there: clutching the window frame, his terrified face pressed against the glass.

Instead, I saw the garden trees being thrashed by rain and wind.

It was a storm and the boy, I suddenly knew, could not survive it. He had called out to me from the end of his endurance.

Where are you? I thought.

I had a murky picture, nothing more. But I knew this: he was crawling. He was crawling somewhere amid the filth of one of Coldharbour's dumps. He'd been dragging his body across the wet rubbish for hours.

Shaking uncontrollably, I checked the clock: gone

midnight. After the commotion I'd made scurrying to the window, I expected Dad to come rushing in—ready to fight, ready for anything—but the storm had masked any sounds from my room. Dad was awake, though.

I wanted to explain to him what had happened, but I hesitated. Something in the boy's cry told me that I must go on my own to find him. Dad wouldn't accept that. He would never let me go out alone to find the boy.

The guest room was open, the light on. To get to the staircase without being seen by Dad I would have to wait until he fell asleep. He didn't even try to sleep, of course. Twice in the next hour he checked on me. Both times I shut my eyes while he stood silently at the door, watching my chest rise and fall. I realized then how far my dad would go to protect me. Wherever he had to. Over the edge of the world.

I waited. I knew he wouldn't truly sleep, but at last the patterns of his mind altered. Just for a moment, he dozed. I slipped straight out of bed, dressed in whatever was easiest to find and tiptoed along the corridor. The guest-room lamp shone at an angle on Dad's face. He lay on the bed, shoes beside him, fully clothed. If the storm hadn't been virtually blowing the house down, I would never have got past without waking him.

All the while I sensed the boy. He was still moving, still slowly crawling across the rubbish and mud of Coldharbour. And then a dread ran through me as I realized: he wasn't using his legs. He was crawling using only his arms;

that's all he had left to move with.

I wasn't thinking properly. To journey on foot through Coldharbour in a storm of this magnitude required heavy walking gear. It required boots, a compass, maps, weatherproof clothing, a strong flashlight, water and food. In my panic I didn't consider any of those things. My light summer jacket was by the front door. I automatically reached for it. My sneakers were still damp from earlier in the day—I put them on. I did think about taking an umbrella, but it meant rummaging under the stairs. That might wake Dad. His mind was already stirring again. I had to leave now, before he discovered me.

Turning the key, I opened the back door as quietly as I could. The creak made almost no noise over the storm. Even so, it was enough to rouse Dad.

"Helen?"

I read his mind—and realized he would check my room before he came downstairs.

That gave me the few extra seconds I needed.

I love you, Dad, I thought. Don't try to follow me.

I ran outside. Utter darkness. Good—once I got away from the house, no one could find me. The dark also meant that every footstep would be treacherous until I reached a road. The nearest was more than a mile away, and I had no idea how to make my way from there to Coldharbour.

Boy, I thought, I'm putting all my trust in you.

The back door banging in the wind drew Dad downstairs. He fumbled for a light. "Helen?" he cried, staggering outside. When I crouched out of sight, offering no answer, he went to find a flashlight.

Dad's mind. It was dreadful to be inside at that moment, because he had no idea what had happened, of course. He thought the boy might have forced his way into the house and taken me against my will. Idiot! Why hadn't I left a note? I couldn't leave him believing that.

"No!" I yelled over the wind. "I'm okay, Dad. It's not that. Let me go."

"Helen?" My words guided him towards me, but I had the advantage. Knowing what direction he would go next, I ran in another, hiding when I needed to from the flashlight. Finally I was too far away for him to pick me out against the darkness.

"Helen! Come back!" he shouted over and over. "What are you doing? Don't run from me! Is it the boy again? I won't stop you going to find him, if that's what it is. Helen, did you hear? Just let me come with you! Helen!"

He continued pleading with me long after I was out of earshot, but at some point he realized that there was a better way to reach me. He stopped shouting. He stopped uselessly waving the flashlight around. He put it down. Standing there in the rain, fear and love choking out of him, Dad gathered his concentration and with all of his mind he reached out to me, promising anything, anything, if I would only return to the house. He was lying, of course. I knew that on a night like this he would never let me out. Until he believed it was safe he would lock me inside, stay on guard forever, bolt every door in the world if he had to.

I'm sorry, Dad, I thought. I have to go. Stay where I know you're safe!

His anguished thoughts gradually faded as I traveled from the house.

Where was I? Somewhere still north of the town, cutting across a field. Dad's mind was no longer with me, but I was not alone, not quite—the animals were there, as always. Some, even in this storm, were burrowing eagerly upwards through the soil, hurrying to feed on whatever might be stranded in the downpour.

And there was something else out there, too—something more distracting than the animals. There it was again, a roar, exactly the same sound that had disturbed me in my room when I lay in bed earlier. But it was clearer now, louder, more confident. This time I didn't have to listen for it. This time it rose up above the storm, and it was like a shriek.

It was like the shriek of a creature that was starving.

I halted, so shocked by it that I nearly turned back.

But the roar was still distant; the boy was closer, and his arms were now barely moving. I continued on, blundering through the darkness, trying to reach him on time. I'd heard nothing at all since his first scream for help sent me scuttling to the window. Why? Could he already be too weak even to cry out to me?

Twice the ferocious wind knocked me down. Each

time I picked myself up and ran on. The rain drove into me, so cold that at one point I pulled the collar of my jacket around my ears. Then I stopped pretending that anything could keep me warm. Ahead, the town lights were hardly visible through the rain.

Beyond them, the bleakness of Coldharbour beckoned to me like a passion.

ELEVEN

the hiss of rain

THOMAS

"Will you two just shut up your racket!"

The twins had been driving me crazy all evening, scratching the door, wanting to be let out—but I wasn't about to go blundering around in Coldharbour during the middle of a storm. I couldn't calm them down, though. Emily was tetchy; Freda simply would not shut up. Around midnight, both stopped arguing with me altogether and simply ran around the shack, going berserk, completely freaking out.

"Just stop it!" I said. "I know you want to go out, but not in this storm!"

"Let uz go!" Emily cried.

"Open the door, Toms!" Freda wailed, slapping my leg.

"Don't be crazy!" I told her. "You'll catch your deaths if you go out in this! Just calm down and tell me what's wrong!"

"There's another special one of 'em out there!"

"Another what?"

"Dunno. Dunno. Let's see!"

The wind hurled rain into the shack. There was no drainage in Coldharbour, nowhere for the water hitting the summer-baked soil to go. Looking through a crack in one of our walls, I could see puddles already turning into lakes big enough to drown in. The twins had given up trying to persuade me. They yanked at the door.

"We'll go out in the morning!" I told them. "Be reasonable! Even if someone's out there, we'll never find them in this."

"Now! Now!"

"The morning!"

Then I heard Walter, banging on the roof. He'd never wanted to come in before, but I suppose even he needed to take shelter from a storm this bad. I held the twins back, but as soon as I opened the door they wriggled past and were out and running.

"Catch hold, Walter!" I yelled, but he simply fell in alongside them, his big arms swinging as the twins scuttled northwards.

"Go on, then!" I shouted. "If you're mad enough to go out there . . . " Cursing them, I went back inside. A moment later Walter was knocking politely on the door. When I didn't answer he pushed it open with his finger, reached in an arm and plucked me up.

"What do you think you're doing?" I demanded, astonished.

"W-w-w-w-we gotta g-go, Tommy," he said apologetically. "I g-got the car door!" He held it over my head, as if that made everything okay.

"Put me down!" I growled. "You should be trying to stop the twins! Who knows what'll happen if they go wandering about in this!"

But something in Walter's expression made me put on a jacket. It was one Emily had found a few weeks earlier. Meant to be waterproof, but it was obviously some cheap rubbish that would leak straight away.

Walter smiled, very satisfied, helping with the hood.

"You look g-good in that," he said, trying to get on the right side of me.

"You great twerp," I said. "Get that door over my head!"

Grinning, Walter plonked me onto his shoulders. He steadied me there with one hand and held the car door at a good angle to the wind. "P-perfect!" he said.

"I'll give you perfect!" I blasted—and then we were off. We were off!

"Whoop! Whoop!" the twins were going, yelping and singing their rhymes. Raindrops bounced off their faces like hail. I'd never seen them so excited, feet and hands racing over the slippery ground, with Walter taking broad strides to keep up.

The girls led us northwest, and after about ten minutes I thought, we can't go on, we just can't. Coldharbour in a downpour: what a mess, all those leftovers from the dumps spilling out over the ground, chasing over your feet. I was quite impressed with Walter, though. He only slipped once, and caught me before I hit the ground. "Flipping idiot!" I shouted, just to make sure he knew how precious his cargo was—not that I needed to.

The conditions got worse, but if anything the twins speeded up. Walter had to leap over ditches and rivers of sludge just to stay with them. Finally we came to a stretch where the water was too deep for even the twins to go any further. They had a chat to Walter. He picked them up and kind of stuck them onto his left shoulder and arm. I was already perched on his right arm. With Walter's hands occupied, we had to get rid of the car door, of course. Walter wasn't happy about that. You should have seen the adoring look he gave that rusty old door. He actually tried putting it between his teeth, then realized it wouldn't work.

Sighing, raising his arms to keep us safe, Walter began wading through the water like some great god of the sea setting out across his domain. Me and the twins were less impressive, bobbing up and down like little kiddies on his shoulders.

What a night! And as soon as we got over the big stretch of water, the twins were off again! There weren't any gang kids about, of course, not in weather like this. I got lost as soon as we left our familiar home patch, but the twins had noses for exactly where they were going. Then, abruptly, they stopped.

There was someone leaning into the wind in front of us.

It was a girl. After Walter, I'd half-expected any new discovery of the twins would turn out to be another giant, but this girl seemed normal enough: average height, about my age, lengthy medium-brown hair. I couldn't tell much else about her because she'd obviously fallen in some of Coldharbour's best filth. What I thought was a misshapen nose turned out to be a blob of mud. I couldn't believe what she was wearing, though—sneakers, a blouse and a flimsy jacket, as if the storm had caught her while on a little stroll to the shops. But she was no scrapper, this one. I could tell straightaway that there was something unusual about her, and it had nothing to do with her appearance.

She hadn't even noticed me. What she had noticed—unmistakably noticed—were the twins sniffing round her feet, and the shape of Walter looming over her like a town. She kept glancing between them in the way I'd seen others do—as if unsure which to concentrate on, who was the most dangerous.

Walter had his own way of greeting people. When he came across them he tried to put them at ease by giving them old lopsided. It didn't normally help much. They usually held up their arms and went "Ugghhhhaaagghhh!" anyway, but this time was different. Once she'd got over the initial shock of seeing him the girl, whoever she was, smiled back and seemed to relax entirely. "Hello,

Walter!" she said, holding out her hand as if she met monster-sized boys like him every day. The effect on Walter was amazing. His face almost exploded with disbelief and happiness. He took her hand as if it was a precious flower, shaking it, virtually wagging her arm off.

"I'm Helen," she said to him, as calmly as you like. "Pleased to meet you. Don't be frightened. I won't hurt you."

I just gaped. Her telling him: *Don't be frightened*? Who *was* this girl?

She bent down to the twins. There's nothing more scary than your first sight of those two fiddling round your ankles—I knew that—but again the new girl was unconcerned. In fact, I thought she was going to pat their heads for a moment. Instead, she just said, "It's not me, is it? You're looking for someone else, aren't you?"

Emily and Freda nodded, their heads up, running all around her.

"Go on," the girl said. "Keep looking. He's here somewhere. I can't find him."

Walter was grinning like a love-struck idiot at the new girl. The twins had run off into the darkness, seemingly happy to do whatever she asked of them. It was hard to look dignified hanging off Walter's arm, but I did my best. "Excuse me . . . Helen, is it?" I said. "Who do you think you are, telling the twins what to do?"

"Oh, I see," she replied, looking at me for the first time. "You think Emily and Freda should be standing beside you, in case I'm dangerous." She shook her head. "You don't even know what's going on, do you? You don't know what the twins are looking for?"

"Do *you* know?" I asked. Then: "Wait a minute! Hold on! How come you know the twins' names? And how do you know Walter?"

Walter put me down and covered Helen with his hands to keep the rain off. I didn't object because she obviously needed it far more than me. What a miserable, drenched state she was in! For a minute Helen simply stood under Walter's fingers while he did his warm-breath trick over her.

Then she laughed. "No," she said to me. "I am definitely not his sister."

"What?" A mad thought had entered my head that somehow she and Walter were part of the same family, with this girl the normal-looking one. "You—you read my thoughts," I whispered. "How . . . did you do that?"

"It's nothing I can teach you," she replied.

And then she gasped. I think she would have fallen over, except that Walter caught her jacket.

"W-w-what's w-wrong?" he asked, wrapping his entire body around her.

Helen looked at me in awe. "*What are you?*" she hissed. "What wonderful thing is in your mind?"

I didn't know what she meant at first, but my beauty did. It opened itself up to her like a flower. Helen tottered back a few steps in amazement. Walter held her upright and, holding onto him, she glanced rapidly between us.

"The roar," she murmured. "So you hear it, too . . . "

I stared at her. "Do you know what it is?"

"No," she said. "I'd hoped you'd be able to explain . . . but you're just as confused as me, aren't you? You've no idea, either . . . "

Walter continued to shield Helen and keep her dry. The twins were still out of sight somewhere behind us. Then I heard them both squeal, followed by silence.

"What's wrong?" I called out.

Emily and Freda tore out of the darkness. Their faces were terrified. I'd never seen the twins look really scared like this before, and they headed straight for Walter. Without hesitation, he gathered them towards him with one arm. With his other arm he picked Helen up. "T-Tommy! Climb on!" he ordered. There was such command in his voice that I obeyed immediately. Like a petrified little kid I scrambled up his legs and perched on his chest.

With Walter holding us all, we waited.

And something emerged from the darkness.

I say something, because what was it? I'd seen the state of some abandoned-looking kids in Coldharbour, but nothing resembling this horror. Was it a boy? If it was, some of him was falling to pieces. His hands were the worst thing. Parts of them were flaking off as I looked at him. As soon as I saw that nausea shuddered through me. I retched. I had to crouch down to contain the pain. At the same time my beauty erupted. Like a force of nature, I felt it burst out of me. "What's . . . happening?" I glanced at Helen, but her eyes were glazed.

"Oh . . . " she murmured, over and over. "Oh . . . "

The twins gripped each other in a fierce embrace. Walter made sure that he held us all securely. My nausea eased off somewhat, and I looked at the creature-boy again. His appearance was beyond belief: golden skin, shining, like a covering of metal, but with one part, on his wrist, a complete contrast: silver, glinting like a furnace.

Emily took my arm. "Ee's saying something!"

It was true. You could see the boy's mouth opening and closing painfully, trying to make a sound. At last he managed to struggle one word past his lips. "M-Milo." He said it once more. Then his throat constricted. You could almost see it collapsing inside his neck.

What kind of boy was this? He couldn't walk; his legs seemed to be useless. And his eyes! No lids! He had no lids with which to blink! His hands were also deformed in some way—I didn't want to look too closely. Everything about him was awful, but the scariest part was the way he moved. Because his legs didn't work, he had to pull himself through the mud on his elbows.

I moved a step towards him—and immediately felt sick again. What was happening? My beauty was reaching out to him, and that was good—I'd *expected* that to happen—but I didn't think it would hurt like this. When my beauty recognized who it was meant to help, I thought the outpouring would feel special for me as well. Instead, I could barely stand. My stomach cramped in agony with every swish forward of Milo's arms.

Helen was staring at him, her mouth wide open. At first I thought she was simply feeling a mixture of pity and disbelief, the same as me. But it was more than that. She was weeping.

"What kind of thing is it?" I demanded. "A boy? Do you know? Is he dangerous?"

"Milo." Walter said the name softly, bending towards the creature-boy. He wanted to help him, at least pick him out of the mud. But Walter wasn't certain he could do so and keep us safe as well.

"Be careful, Walts," Freda said.

The boy steadily swished his way towards us. I could hardly believe that anyone so injured could move at all. As he drew closer I could hear his labored breathing.

Helen started to moan, holding her head. "Don't, don't, don't!"

"What's the matter?" I said.

"He's . . . " She couldn't speak.

"Can you read his thoughts?" I shouted at her. "What's wrong with him?"

The boy continued to head towards us. Emily and Freda gripped each other more tightly. All my Coldharbour-trained instincts told me that we should keep our distance. "Don't let that thing near us, Walter!" I said. "I mean it."

The boy wriggled forward. It was terrible for all of us to watch, but the girl Helen was in absolute torment. She sobbed and sobbed. Then, just before the boy reached us, an extraordinary thing took place: some rain, splattering on his eyes, sizzled. Seeing that, even Walter took a step back.

"Flipping heck!" I whispered. I suddenly felt sick again, and retched several times. "What's wrong with him?" I shouted at Helen.

Tears were falling steadily down her face.

"He's altering," she choked out. "He's . . . he's *changing*."

Walter reached out to help the boy. I flailed at his hand. "You idiot!" I bellowed. "He might have a disease, something contagious!"

Helen's eyes were pools. "It's not that," she said. "Milo . . . he can't . . . he can't . . . he can't . . . can't . . . breathe!" She swallowed hard, as if in great pain herself. "Oh, he's in torment. His legs . . . are a dead weight to him . . . his brain is going mad trying to stop the pain, but nothing . . . can fight this much. His heart . . . " She couldn't go on.

I turned to stare at him. "Milo," I whispered.

He was nearer to us now, mouth open, gulping for air. His hands were like red wrecks. He held them out to Helen, as if he wanted her to pick him up and take him away from all this.

"I . . . " Helen backed away. "I can't . . . stand it . . . I can't . . . "

"What does he expect from us?" I demanded. "Helen! What's going on?"

The boy was so close now that we could hear for ourselves what Helen had been trying to tell us about his heart. What a force! It was stronger than ours. You could hear it beating from his chest, a mighty nerve-jangling thump. His head continued to hiss softly when the rain struck it.

Suddenly I could see that Helen was losing it. She stepped away from the boy. "Stop it!" She held her head as if to shut him out. "I can't . . . take . . . it's too much! I'm . . . burning . . . I'm burning to death!"

She screamed, slipped from Walter's grip, and ran away into the night.

"Don't-g-go!" begged Walter. "H-Helen!" He seemed about to launch off after her, but Milo held out his stubs of hands to us, and Walter stopped.

"Toms, help 'im!" Freda was saying. "Do something!"

"All right," I said, trying to think. I was mixed up about the boy, much more nervous of him than Walter or the twins. Why couldn't he just say more, help me to trust him? Another cramp of sickness welled up in me. Walter knelt beside Milo. "What are you doing?" I said. "Don't touch him!"

"He's s-sick," Walter said.

"I know he's sick! You heard Helen. He's changing into something else. Who knows what!" I heard my voice rising out of control, but I couldn't stop myself. I was so scared! For some reason, Milo frightened me half to death. "Look at him!" I said. "Is that a boy? Is it human? All that gold! I'm not sure . . . "

"Poor harmed thing," Freda murmured, bending towards him.

"Don't!" I said.

"We gotta do something!" Emily demanded.

Then Milo smiled at us—an actual smile.

Putting me and the twins down, Walter went to pick him up. It was not clear how to safely do so. Walter gently explored his body, searching for soft spots and harder ones. Experimentally, he tried moving one of Milo's arms. A cracking sound made him stop at once—a bone broken. Walter glanced desperately at me. I had no idea what to say. In the end Walter simply scooped the entire boy up in his great palms, trying to figure out what to do next.

The twins waited near him anxiously.

Milo was looking at me. He smiled again. He lay like a madman's misshapen doll in Walter's hands, smiling at me as if I was Santa Claus or something! An awful pain made me shudder again. I doubled up, retching over and over.

"Where are you from?" I asked him. "What are you?"

He didn't answer. I don't think he was able to. He just kept smiling at me gravely, as if it was me who needed help, not him.

The twins skittered up to me. I knew what they were going to say.

"Oh, no!" I told them. "Out of the question! No way. I'm not having that in the shack!"

"Take 'im! Take 'im!" The twins started up an almighty wailing.

"You gots to, Toms!"

"Heal 'im! You can do it, Toms!"

"I can't heal him!" I said. "I can't!"

"Bring 'im back then. *We'll* look after 'im. We'll heal 'im!"

"Heal how?" I protested.

Walter stared at me. "Tommy, you c-can't . . . you can't . . . just leave him o-o-out h-here."

What was I going to do? I looked at Milo, covered in rain, steam rising from his boiling face. I looked at the twins, rubbing my hands and feet, trying to persuade me. Did they think I had no pity for the boy? Of course I did!

"Bring him then," I said, "but . . . I'm not touching him, and he stays outside the shack, not in it. Do you understand?"

Walter nodded, and was about to set off when he frowned. "C-can't c-carry him," he said.

"What do you mean?" I asked.

"Rain's w-worse. Can't h-hold Milo and you all as well."

Walter glanced at the twins and they understood at once. Taking a deep breath, each of the girls stood on the soles of their feet. For a few moments they practiced moving cooperatively in an upright way together, their arms held like a cradle. With the utmost care Walter distributed Milo's weight between them.

Then, arranging the twins and Milo onto his left side, and me on his right, Walter started off. He took one careful step at a time, to avoid shaking the boy too much.

I clung to Walter the whole way. I didn't even complain, I was so miserable from all the rain and cold. I could hardly look at Milo. Why did he scare me so much?

A long journey, but eventually we made it back. The twins immediately took the boy inside the shack. "No! No!" I said. "Leave him out!" But they weren't listening to me. Nobody seemed to be tonight, and I was too weary to argue. I slumped in a corner of the shack as far away from the boy as possible, watching as the girls dried him off.

Milo, I thought, trying to get used to the unusual sound of his name. Milo.

The twins attempted to dribble some water down his lips. Milo didn't want it. They tried to give him a bite to eat, but he just twisted his head away. So instead Freda got out my mattress and carefully put the boy down on the cleanest sheet.

"They're mine!" I said. "What are you doing?"

"'Ave a heart," Emily said, ashamed of my behavior.

Milo lay there wretchedly, boiling-skinned, steaming up the shack, his monumental heart slamming away. Every time he shuddered tiny bits of skin flaked off his hands, like pollen in a wind. It was horrible. I turned away. I'd never felt offended by the sight of anything so much in my whole life.

Walter prodded me.

"Leave me alone!" I said.

Angrily Freda grabbed my face, twisted it, made me look at the boy.

"If you'd a kindness, you'd give it 'im," she said. "If you'd a care! Go on, Tommy. Give 'im some of it. Give 'im some o' yer beauty."

"Just shut up!" I whined. "I let you bring him back, didn't I? Just be grateful for that! He's got my bed! I'm not giving him anything else, do you hear?"

The twins looked at me with contempt, but they didn't understand. I didn't want to tell them yet, because I didn't know what it meant myself. You see, I was already giving Milo all my beauty. From the first moment I saw him the beauty had been flowing out of me and into him like a tide.

TWELVE

storm

HELEN

I ran into the storm, trying to find a way back to Dad.

Milo—a boy's name. I ran from whatever he was. Ridiculous! As if he could catch me! As if a wounded boy propelled only by his arms could catch me!

Finally, to get my breath and make certain I was alone, I stopped running. As soon as I did, I felt the rain cooling me. Cooling me? No, I realized: that was what Milo had felt; he had felt such relief when the rain splashed against his hot skin. I was still experiencing his pain.

Oh, what was he? I don't know what I'd expected, but not him, or anything like him. I knew he would be different, knew that he would be in need, but not that much need. I felt seared by contact with him. I felt scorched.

I'd expected a golden boy, not something that reached down inside me to burn!

And now I was lost in a storm in Coldharbour. No roads here, no landmarks to show the way home. The boy had led me to him, but where had I run to? The landscape was black all around, except for rare flashes of lightning shooting silently down the sky, followed by thunder. All I could see in those brief lit-up moments was rain, rain hitting me in the face, rain churning up the earth, or erupting in filthy rivulets around my feet.

My hopeless jacket was no protection at all. How could I have left home on a night like this dressed in next to nothing? But I knew how. The boy—only a short while ago, nothing would have kept me away from him. Even now blasts of wind kept sweeping into my face, as if they hated me for abandoning him. Is that what I'd done? Abandoned him? But look what he'd done to me! Look how he'd terrified me!

That wasn't why I left home to be with him!

In the distance I could see smeary illuminations—the town lights. To reach them I had to face into the brunt of the storm. I don't know how long I blundered that way, but eventually I just couldn't bear to walk into those gusts anymore. I turned and leaned my back against the wind—as if it might hold me up, the way Walter had done.

That astonishing boy! What a different mind, what a treasure he was. Walter had no selfish thoughts, just an overwhelming concern for me and everyone else. As for the twins, I saw immediately how they were driven to search for exceptional children. That was their purpose, and had I stayed with them longer I might have learned something about dedication.

Thomas was different. I'd nearly cried when I first saw him, because for a moment I thought he was my boy—the one who had led me all this way. Toms, the twins called him. That wasn't a lovely enough name for the beauty in his mind. What extraordinary gift was it? And what was linking Thomas with Milo? If I'd stayed I might have found out. But I couldn't have stayed for another second so close to that much pain!

I staggered on into the storm. There were vague shapes in the rainy darkness. At one point I passed a hut. Inside there was a crackle of light. If I'd been thinking straight, I would have listened in on the minds of those within, and might have found some kindness there. Instead, I kept moving. On and on, constantly falling over and getting up.

The town lights seemed no closer, and at some point I stopped searching for them altogether. I turned in another direction—anything to get relief from the wind! The next time I looked up there was no light anywhere to guide me. I struggled on, with no idea where I was, just trying to keep in a straight line. At last I glanced down at my feet. They weren't moving anymore. I'd stopped walking. When had that happened? Frightened, I tottered a little further. Finally I slipped and hit the ground hard, catching my cheek on a sharp object. I didn't realize there was a cut at first; my face was too numb to feel it. Then I noticed the blood, warmer than rain, flowing down my cheek.

Dad, I thought, help me.

"Up!" I shouted at myself. "Get up! Keep moving, Helen!"

I struggled upright, managed to stand. Into the storm again, a few more steps. And then I simply couldn't anymore. All I could think about was hiding from the wind and cold. Not lying down—not quite giving up completely—I sat on the ground, drew my jacket around my face and tried to find a place inside my blouse to protect my hands. I don't know how long I stayed that way. I lost track of time. After a while my hands stopped feeling cold altogether. I could hold them into the wind and they felt no worse. I knew that was bad, but I didn't have the energy to get up again. My mind started to drift. An image of Dad came to my mind, a stupid picture of him finding me, carrying me home and locking the windows and doors against all our enemies. Time passed, and I wanted more than anything to sleep—but I knew what would happen if I did. A tiny instinct of self-preservation made me keep my eyes open. I was no longer able to struggle against the cold, or anything else. I sensed the animals around me. Some were dying in this storm. Others were feeding. I gazed around, like one of the unfortunate ones, like an animal that was only capable, in its final moments, of looking around to see what would take advantage of it.

Then I felt a tremor. In the darkness behind me the earth shook, and even in my wretched state I discovered a vestige of strength to be able to crawl away from whatever it was.

But he took me in his arms, and as he lifted me up he examined the blood on my cheek.

"Who has d-done this to you?" Walter thundered.

The wind ceased. Walter's body canceled it out. Like a little rag of wetness I curled up inside his denim-patched jacket, clutching for his warmth. For a time we said nothing. Walter just held me. Then he gave me a cautious smile, lifted an immense finger and used it to gently clean the muck from my face.

His mind—I can't describe how wonderful it was to be inside there.

Walter examined me to ensure that I had no major injuries. The bone of Milo—the one that had snapped when he lifted him—still bothered Walter deeply. He believed some clumsiness of his own had been responsible.

"You didn't do it," I said. "The boy's body— it's . . . changing so much."

Walter nodded, tears flowing down his face. "N-not f-fair, Helen," he said. "Got to d-do s-something for him. G-got to."

Experiencing Walter's overwhelming concern for Milo, I felt ashamed. But I also knew this: even if Milo was here with us now, I'd run a second time. I wasn't ready to face him again. I doubted I ever would be.

"Pardon m-me," Walter said. Gathering up my drenched hair, he wrung it out like a towel. Then he winked at me. "Cl-close your eyes." I knew what he was going to do and shut my lids tight. His breath ran over me like summer.

Realizing how incredible it was, I asked Walter how he found me.

"K-knew you would n-never g-get home, not in this," he replied.

I looked into his mind, and saw journeys. Walter hadn't known where to find me. He had just looked everywhere without stopping until he did.

"Can you . . . would you take me home?" I asked him.

Walter's mind blazed with hope. He thought I'd made a choice to return with him to Tommy, the twins and Milo.

"It's not f-far, Helen!" he cried, ready to set off at once. "Not far at-at all! We—"

"No," I said, feeling awful. "I didn't mean that, Walter. I meant—to my real home, where my dad is. He'll be worried about me."

"Oh . . . " Walter tried to hide his disappointment. "C-course, Helen. C-c-course I'll t-take you." He buried his hopes, concentrating instead on what to do for me. When I told him how far away I lived, Walter shook his head. He didn't want to carry me so far in my exhausted state. An idea struck him. He liked it. He gave me a big grin, tucked me inside his jacket, and bounded south-wards.

It was the wrong way, but I knew what Walter intended.

A run-down bungalow came into view, isolated on the outskirts of Coldharbour. Walter knocked diffidently, and put on his best face for whoever lived there. I could read the mind of the man inside. He lived alone, and was nervous even before he saw us. Of course, when he opened the door a crack and saw Walter he nearly wet himself.

Walter asked—cordially—if he had a fire. With all the blood draining from his face, the man managed to nod, and backed away as Walter squeezed his way in.

"Th-thanks. Fr-freezing out there," Walter said, by way of explanation. "I'm w-w-w—" He sighed, started again. "I'm w-w-Walter—don't mind me." He shook the man's hand, rolling his eyes in apology at his own immense proportions.

The man just blinked at him, wondering if this was the night he was going to die.

There was an electric three-bar fire in the room.

"Excuse m-me," Walter said. All this time he'd been hiding me inside his jacket. The man had no idea I was there. Now Walter unbuttoned, brought me out and held me next to the fire.

"No!" screamed the man. For a moment he thought Walter was going to roast me.

Walter was taken aback. "I w-won't hurt you," he said hurriedly. Then he started turning me so that the left and right sides of my body got an equal amount of heat. He smiled his very best at the man. "Have y-you got any c-clothes? For H-Helen, I mean." Walter turned my face towards the man, in case he had any doubt who Helen was. "She's cold," Walter explained. "She n-needs to change."

A look of relief came over the man. He rummaged around and found some old jeans, a shirt, a coat too. Walter helped me take off my waterlogged shoes and socks. The man was still wide-eyed, but beginning to recover some of his composure. "You want a towel, too?" he asked. "I've got towels."

"Thanks," Walter said, shaking his hand again.

When the man fetched them I slipped from Walter's arms, went into a corner and changed into the rough new clothes. They didn't fit, of course, but I didn't care—it was just so good to feel dry again! For a while I simply lay near the fire, stretching out my feet, recovering.

"N-nice place you have h-here," Walter noted, glancing round.

"Nice of you to say so," the man answered. He seemed to understand by now that Walter wouldn't harm him. He offered me some sandwiches, which I ate gratefully. "Want a drink as well, love?" he asked. "Something hot? I've got tea."

"Thank you," I said.

"G-got any h-hot chocolate?" Walter asked shyly.

The man half-grinned. "Yeah, I've got that, too." He went into his kitchen to make the drinks, and when he came back we all sat around the fire sipping away, as if we did this every night. "You've been out in this storm, have you?" the man ventured. "What on earth for?"

Then it just tumbled out of Walter, didn't it, the whole night: finding Milo, his appalling injuries, Tommy sick and scared of him, and Walter helpless, not knowing what to do. And as Walter stuttered out the story, I could sense an incredible thing happening to the man beside us. He'd been living on his own for years on the edge of Coldharbour, just trying to hold himself together on next to nothing, and suddenly here was Walter, so genuine, so anxious about someone else's life, that the man felt this wonderful desire to reach out and help. It caught him completely by surprise.

"Tell me what I can do?" he offered. "You want me to talk to your Tommy lad? Would that help?"

"You've done so much already," I said to him. "We're really grateful." I nudged Walter, sensing it would be a mistake to get this well-intentioned man involved.

"Y-yeah, we should g-go," Walter said apologetically.

"Stay as long as you like," the man said, as Walter and I stood up—and he meant it. "No bother to me. You're welcome, both of you."

But Walter wanted to leave as well, fearing what might happen if he didn't return quickly to the shack. He'd only waited this long to give me a chance to recover. As he got up from the floor, stooping to avoid the ceiling, he said to the man, "Poor th-thing, Milo—his legs, they d-don't work, you know."

We stepped outside. The rain had stopped, but the night wind was still fierce.

"If you need anything, come back," the man said. "By the way, my name's Stan."

I knew, of course, but hadn't wanted to frighten him by letting on.

"I'll bring back the clothes," I told him.

"Don't worry about it, young lady," Stan said. "Are you sure you don't need anything else?"

"No, really," I said. "I'll be fine. Walter will look after me now."

As we left, Walter shook the man's hand several more times, and Stan—touched deeply by him—waved us off until we were out of sight.

With me hidden away inside his jacket, Walter set off. Using tremendous strides he crossed the river, avoided the town center, and headed north. I got my bearings and was able to direct him up the steep fields leading towards the house.

Home. I looked up. All the lights were on—Dad trying to make it as easy as possible for me to find my way back. He stood in the living room, talking with someone on the phone—the police, I realized.

Walter smiled at me. "That's your d-dad, is it?" I knew in that moment he had no memory of his own father. Walter's thoughts didn't linger there. He was anxious to return to his duties in Coldharbour.

"Y-you're safe now," he said, putting me down. "You're

h-home, aren't you?"

"Yes," I said.

He gazed at me.

"I have to go," I said.

He nodded.

"Please . . . take care of yourself, Walter," I whispered. Pathetic—as if I had nothing more to say than that to the boy who had just saved my life! Actually, I wanted to say much more, but I didn't dare encourage Walter into thinking I would return to Coldharbour. That's what he hoped; secretly Walter hoped that once I recovered from the shock of whatever Milo had done to me, I'd come back to help. *Take care of yourself* wasn't enough, though. I tugged at Walter's jacket to bring him down. As he bent over I reached up on my toes and kissed that massive bony cheek of his.

He stared at me, embarrassed and happy. "Y-you don't have to help with the b-boy M-Milo if you're s-scared of him," he said. "Of c-course not! He . . . m-might not need that much, m-me and Emms and F-Freda can do it. You c-could just come b-back, m-maybe t-talk to Tommy, and—"

"No," I said. "Walter, please . . . I can't . . . "

"N-not now!" Walter exploded, smiling away. "Not yet! Of course n-not now! You n-need to see your dad! But . . . when you're b-better, you—"

"Walter, don't . . . "

He suddenly got down on his knees. "P-please come

back, Helen," he begged. "I c-can't do it on m-my own. I can't!"

"I'm too scared, Walter. Don't you understand!"

"I'm s-scared, too!" he said. "It's all right t-t-to be scared, Helen. You can still d-do things! Even if you-you-you're s-scared to, you can."

I shook my head, tears falling down my face. When Walter saw that it was too much for him. "Nah, nah," he said, managing a tortured smile. "N-never mind. B-better go."

He checked the cut on my cheek one last time. Then, making sure I could stand upright without his help, he raced away into what was left of the night.

THIRTEEN

monster

THOMAS

Milo lay on my mattress, falling to pieces.

He hadn't said a single word since the twins carried him into the shack, though he'd tried hard enough. In a world of pain he was, you could see that, but somehow he still managed a glance of gratitude for the efforts of the twins. For hours they'd been all over him with their care, propping him up with bits of foam, and cleaning him up where he'd let them.

"I got hands all right," Freda murmured to me, "but what to do with 'em, Toms—that's a different matter! Look at Milo, just burning away like soon there'll be nothin' left of 'im at all, wiv his arms all twisted up. We gotta find a way to give 'im a bit more comfort and respect." She tucked a blanket over Milo's exposed foot, then said to Emily, "Ee's a sorry sight, lying in bed wivout any clothes to his name. Even though we'd probably crack his bones to get a shirt on, I think ee'd like it, Emms."

"Maybe," Emily replied softly. "Not yet, though, eh? Just talk softly wiv 'im; ee don't seem to want anything else right now."

"His breathing's eased up anyways," Freda said, trying to convince herself. "And ee's not so sad-looking, is ee?"

Walter, who had recently returned from Helen's house, offered Freda an encouraging smile, but he didn't really mean it. Both he and I could see that there had been no improvement in Milo. The twins did their best, but they'd try one thing to ease Milo's body, then some other part of him would snap, and we'd just have to close our eyes and hope. The noises coming from him! Even when the twins weren't anywhere near Milo, the splintering and collapsing sounds from his body were enough to keep us all on edge.

Walter raised the question of the hospital, but only feebly. We all realized that whatever ailed our Milo couldn't be fixed by doctors.

Milo needed my beauty.

And wasn't I the one to give it? Wasn't I the one person who could help him? I knew that was true, but I was still frightened of him. The beauty was pouring into him, and I kept wanting to hold some of it back. The twins and the shivering girl I'd met on the northern dump had only needed a flicker of my beauty. Milo wanted so much! He was taking it all! And on top of everything else, I felt ill. Maybe I'd caught some kind of virus—either that or being out in the storm had really wiped out all my strength. Whatever it was, I could only lie there exhausted, my entire body itching and aching.

Throughout the day Milo continued to change. Freda remained optimistic, but there was no pretending that his arms would ever be like ours again. The upper parts could no longer move; they were fixed like bone against his chest. His hands were no better, either; some fingers were missing, and those remaining were deformed.

But I think the temperature was probably the hardest thing to bear. Milo's body never stopped pumping out great chunks of heat. At the same time his golden skin continued to peel away. Something else lay under that gold, a brighter substance. I wished he would talk. Why couldn't he just say a few words, anything to make him seem more like one of us? It wouldn't have been so bad if he hadn't kept staring at me—but there was no escaping those lidless eyes!

During the night I kept falling into feverish dreamy sleeps. One time I woke up, and a lot of time must have passed because the storm had abated and the sun was out. I felt so hot! I considered leaving the shack—just to get some air—but felt sick as soon as I tried to move.

"What is the *matter* with me?" I cried out. "What's going on?"

Emily scampered over, offering some water. She put a hand against my temple.

"You don't look right, Toms, that's true," she said worriedly. "A bit o' fever you got."

I let her cool me down with a damp cloth, and felt slightly better afterwards. After that, I drifted off to sleep again. Sometime later Freda's voice woke me.

"Eh, look," she was whispering. "Ee's . . . doing something!"

I glanced across. Milo had managed to prop himself up on one arm. With his other arm he awkwardly reached out for a nearby cup of water.

"You want a drink now?" Freda asked gently. "You didn't want it before. You want it now, eh? You thirsty?" She put the cup to his lips, but Milo shook his head.

"Ee wants to do it himself, don't ee," Emily said, understanding. "Ee wants a bit o' dignity. Ah, here yer goes." She handed him the cup. Briefly what was left of Milo's bandaged fingers closed around the handle. He clenched it. We could all see how much he wanted to be able to do just this one small thing for himself. But as he brought it towards his mouth, the cup slipped. It clattered against his chest. Milo's skin sizzled as the water splashed over it. Tears appeared at the corners of his eyes. They evaporated at once, and Milo turned his face sadly into the mattress.

"Ah, yer poor thing," Freda said. "If I'd a way, I'd dry yer tears."

"If I'd a way," Emily added in an undertone, "I'd end yer fears."

Milo let out a small cry, then choked it back. He actually tried to gulp back his own tears. I stared at him, then.

You could see how humiliating it was for him to be like this in front of us, so helpless, so incapacitated. He attempted to pull an edge of the sheet closer around him, but even that was beyond his weak grip. Emily did it instead, but when she bent her face to say a few nice words to him Milo just shuffled lower. He crept under the sheets until his head was entirely hidden. The twins both fussed over him for a few minutes, but he wouldn't come out.

"Ee sat up by himself, though!" Freda said, ever hopeful. "That's definitely improvement!"

I wasn't so sure. As Milo slid under the sheets, I'd noticed only a small difference—the silver area on his wrist had gleamed more strongly than all the gold. Was that an improvement?

After another period of dozing off and on, I woke to find myself gasping for breath. Walter was beside me at once, offering a sip of water. I could barely swallow it.

"What is the matter with me!" I shouted. "I feel terrible! I'm worse than *him!*"

Emily rushed over. "Give yerself some of your own beauty, Toms," she said. "Why don't yer? A nub of it, just enough to strengthen yerself."

I tried—and heard Milo scream.

We locked eyes. Milo was sitting up, unaided. He looked stronger as well; while I'd been sleeping there had been some real progress in his condition. It was then I sensed how little of my beauty was left. I looked at the healthier Milo, even now drawing it out of me, and suddenly I thought with horror: is that why I'm so weak and ill? Because all my beauty is pouring into you?

"What are you doing to me?" I screamed.

I dragged myself from the floor across to him. Walter came between us.

"D-don't hurt him, Tommy."

"Me hurt *him*?" I said. "Look at me! I'm a wreck! I can't manage anything! Walter . . . he's . . . he's done something to me, I'm certain of it! All my beauty's going into him! I can't stop it! The longer he's here, the worse I feel. He's—"

"Calm down, Toms," Freda said firmly. "You don't know what yer saying. Milo wouldn't hurt anyone. Yer sick that's all, it's the fever."

"It's not the fever," I said, pointing at Milo. "No one else's got it, have they? Don't you understand? It's *him*. It must be! What is he? A boy? Convince me! Look at his skin, his throat! Look at those eyes!"

Emily said, "Toms, ee's still a boy! Ee cries like one, even if his tears can't make it past his eyes wivout drying out. Ain't that a human thing?"

Before I could answer, there was a noise behind us— Milo. One of his hands scrabbled wildly in the air.

"What is it?" Freda asked him. "You want a bite to eat now?" She offered a biscuit. "This? You hungry?" Milo grasped the biscuit. Then, crushing it, he dropped the pieces down his throat.

"What the—" I gasped, and at last even Walter and the twins were truly afraid, because there was nothing normal about the way Milo ate that biscuit. The inside of his throat was like a hollow tube. He pushed the biscuit fragments down his tube-throat. When they disappeared—without needing to be swallowed—his hand flapped about for more.

The twins, scared stiff, started passing him whatever they could find. Old bread, vegetables, turkey. Milo ate everything, not even looking at what they were giving him. Maybe he had a great storage area down there instead of a stomach! Walter and I looked on in disbelief as he dumped the food down his gullet, without so much as a gulp or smack of his lips. Milo only made one sound—a piercing moan if the twins delayed getting the next batch of food to him. He couldn't wait! Even the superfast twins were hardly able to keep up with his needs. Within minutes almost all our stocks were gone.

"Stop!" I screamed, seeing his skin alter in color. "No more feeding! He needs the food to help him change!"

Walter and the twins gave me a blank stare.

"He's transforming!" I said. "We don't know what he's changing into, do we? He's bad enough now. What if it's into something less human than he already is?"

The food had run out. For a moment Milo squealed, then something else happened: his entire face flashed silver. His back also bulged, a ghastly movement. Then both changes subsided, and Milo lay down again.

"There wasn't enough," I whispered, trying to understand. "That's it! Don't you see? He's not a boy—or, if he ever was, he's turning himself into something else. And we're helping! By looking after him, by feeding him up, all we're doing is helping him turn faster into a beast!"

The twins were listening closely to me. Walter seemed less sure.

"Just look at him!" I said to Walter. "No boy could eat as much as he just did! When you were changing, did you ever eat like that? Well?" Walter shook his head. "Exactly. None of us did. He's not like us, not at all. Listen to that heart banging away! You can barely hear anything else! A boy's body doesn't need a heart that size. I think he's becoming something terrible . . . a monster . . . "

"N-no, no," Walter said, placing his hands on me. "Y-you're safe. We can g-get away. He c-can't h-hurt us, Tommy. M-Milo c-can't hardly move his legs. H-how can he hurt us?"

"He doesn't need to *run* after us," I said. "I'm telling you, he's draining all my beauty. You're next, probably. You're useful to him now, he knows that, protecting him, feeding him up like a beast, he needs it, but I'm on to him, the only one of us, and he knows! Maybe that's why he's taking my beauty, trying to get rid of me . . . "

"Stop ranting!" Freda said sharply. "No one told uz this was going to be easy! Whatever's happening to you . . . I dunno . . . it must be some kind of normal infection. Toms, listen—"

"It's not an infection!" I shouted. "Not a virus-thing, not an infection! *He's* doing it! Deliberately. Look at him! People don't glow gold or silver, no matter what kind of disease they've got!" I backed away from Milo. "I won't stay in this shack with him anymore. Get him out! Get him out of here!"

"*Y-you* get out," Walter said, suddenly angry with me. "Until you calm down. G-go on!"

"What? Me?" I couldn't believe it. Why couldn't Walter see what was taking place here?

"M-Milo'll most likely die if you don't still h-help him," he said. "You've g-got to!"

I said nothing.

"Do you w-want him to d-die, Tommy?"

The shack became silent, except for Milo's ragged breathing.

"What a thing to say!" I replied. "What made you say that?"

Walter looked right at me. "You d-don't care much though, do you?"

"What?" I couldn't believe Walter had said that. His words upset me more than I was willing to show. "All right!" I shouted, covering up my feelings. "Have it your way! Wait till he sucks the life out of you!" I struggled to get up. Without help from Walter, or anyone else, I pushed open the door of the shack and staggered out.

I sat down in the mud outside, trying to think.

No more rain, thank goodness. The sky was clear, with the reek of all the rubbish of Coldharbour stinking up the air after the storm. It made me want to gag—as if I wasn't sick enough already! How ill was I? I forced myself to stand, but barely managed a couple of wobbly steps before I collapsed again.

Walter immediately left the shack and hovered nearby. Evidently he'd been watching me.

"Go away!" I told him. "I'm sick of the sight of you! Go back inside! Back to Milo—isn't that what you really want?"

"N-no. That's n-not true, Tommy, y-you know—"

"All right," I snapped, feeling too ill to fight anymore. Actually, I wanted peace again between me and Walter, not arguments. If only I didn't feel so awful! What crazy thing was wrong with me that *everything* had to hurt so much? I had a headache bad enough to make me want to cry, but I didn't have time for that, did I? I had to figure out what was going on here.

Milo. Was he really doing this to me? I'd lost my head back there in the shack, but it wasn't all just in my feverish imagination. His throat! And, I remembered now, Helen had been frightened of him, too. She could read minds; she probably knew exactly what was going on inside Milo's head. Was that why she'd run from him, even into that awful storm?

I glanced across at Walter. After one of his usual security checks round the neighborhood, he'd edged closer, ready to catch me if I keeled over. As always he kept one anxious eye on me, the other looking out for dangers that might be approaching from the world at large.

Walter, me, the twins, Helen—and the mysterious Milo.

What was going on between us all? I thought about Walter, those massive haunches of his. And the twins: all that spindly-speed and smell-sense. All three of them were special types of children. I, too, had a gift, my beauty. We were, as Freda said often enough, a sort of family. I even think the girl Helen belonged with us. I'd had that feeling the second I saw her.

Then Milo had come along. Everything had been fine until he swished on his arms out of the darkness!

What was *he*? Just desperate and in trouble? Someone to be pitied, to be helped? I'd thought so at first. But when you looked at what had taken place, wasn't it obvious what he was? Hadn't he latched himself onto me from the start? Hadn't I felt sick the moment I set eyes on him, as if I already knew? The second he saw me he attacked, sucking at my beauty! I didn't mind at first, but he never stopped taking it! And now, when I had virtually nothing left, he was still taking it! I'd been ill since he came into my life, and now I was so ill that I could hardly walk! Every second I felt worse.

Was Milo some type of parasite, living off my beauty? Like a kind of cuckoo-child, I thought. He's like a cuckoo, being fed, growing stronger on the food of others, until at some point he's ready to push everyone out of the nest! Perhaps, I thought, he uses everyone—or maybe he just seeks out the ones like me.

Emily handed a jacket to Walter from the shack. He crept up behind me and arranged it around my shoulders. "You f-feeling better, Tommy? N-not too cold? Don't w-want to g-go back inside?"

"I'm fine," I murmured, so locked into my ideas that I barely heard him. Could I be wrong about Milo? But look at what he'd done since he arrived! The rest of us supported each other, but all Milo did was take! At first it seemed that he belonged with us, but that was obviously just part of his trickery. He knows exactly what he's doing, I thought. First he takes my beauty, using it to strengthen himself. Then, to make sure that I don't catch on, he acts the part of a disfigured boy, when underneath it all he's changing into what he wants to be. By the time I realize the truth, it's too late. He's won Walter over, he's won the twins over; while I'm eking out my final dying breaths it's him they're surrounding to protect, not me.

I trembled slightly, thinking about it.

Was it him or me? Was it as basic as that? Yes, I thought. I'd been stupid shouting my head off in the shack. Now Milo knew I was on to him, and would probably try to finish me off even more quickly. I'll have to get rid of him, I thought. Not kill him, of course. Not unless I had no choice. But I had to do something fast. How long would it be before I was too weak even to lift my body off the floor?

I took several shallow, painful lungfuls of air. Whatever I decided to do, it wouldn't be easy. There was no point trying to convince Walter or the twins to help me. Milo already had them wrapped around his lack of fingers! Whatever needed to be done, I'd have to do it myself.

"I'm ready to go back in now," I said to Walter. I gave him a smile, but it was so long since he'd seen one from me that I think it just made him suspicious. As soon as he helped me inside the whiff of decay hit me from Milo's body.

The twins were crying.

"What's wrong?" I asked, moving across to them.

"Ee's been so much worse since you went out," Emily said. "Ee can't seem to bear it wivout your beauty close by."

Of course he needs me close, I thought. Easier to take the beauty that way! I stared coldly at him.

"Ee's been trying to talk as well," Freda said. "Throat's just not right for it anymore, though. Ee can hardly do it. But ee's been trying to say something."

"Well, like what?" I asked, pretending to be interested.

"Your name, we thinks," Freda said.

"My name?"

"Ee did it before, too. Earlier, when you was asleep. Ee's been trying to say it to you all day, last night as well."

I edged closer to Milo—not too close—and looked at him. What a state! What a hideous state! Then suddenly—it was amazing—he reached out with his stubs and tried to grab me. I slapped him back, as if he was a spider jumping on my hand. "Don't you touch me, you freak!" I yelled. "Don't—"

"Th-th-th–" he was going. "Th-th–"

His eyes were pleading with me. I hated him, but even I couldn't look into those eyes without feeling something. Whatever he was doing to me, his suffering was real enough, you couldn't have any doubt about that. He managed to sit upright and take a half-clear breath. "Th-than-thank-thank-you thank you," he whispered, in an agony to get out the words, nearly passing out with the pain of it. "I-I-I-I'd be g-gone now. By now I would. Only you are keeping me alive with your beauty, Thomas. Bless you."

He fell back on the bed, almost dead with the effort of those words, and the twins had nothing on me for tears, did they? All my plans to get rid of him went out of the window, and I just held his rags of hands and cried and cried.

a b a n d o n m e n t

HELEN

Dad ran down the garden path, my oversized clothes sparking off all kinds of wild thoughts in him.

"It's all right," I said. "I borrowed these, and no one's coming after me."

"Are you sure?"

"Yes."

I think Dad almost wanted an attacker to chase off, something physical to confront—but it wouldn't be that easy, would it? He carried me into the house, and I didn't object. After running away, I'd been preparing myself for his anger. How stupid of me! There was only a single emotion shooting through Dad—relief, his sheer relief at finding me alive. It made me weep, because I'd felt that same relief before.

The first time he saw me, as he lay there in the mud, I'd felt it from Milo.

Not wanting to think about that, I asked for a few

moments of privacy, sloped upstairs and took a long, long shower. When I dressed and came down I noticed that Dad had locked the doors and windows against all our enemies. There was soup on the dining table, some coffee as well. The fire was lit, making the room slightly too warm—which felt right after so much coldness. Outside, the sun shone down through a sky full of birds searching for morsels uncovered by last night's storm. I closed my eyes, not wanting their appetites today.

Dad poured the coffee, watching me closely. In his mind I saw the missing person report he'd filed with the authorities. Of course, they hadn't known where to look.

"I've phoned the police to say you're back," he said. "And if you're reading my mind, you'll know the question I have is, should I be telling them anything else? Someone to go after, I mean?"

"No," I said, "I don't think so." Even if I could find my way around Coldharbour without Milo, I knew it wasn't help from the police he needed.

"Well," Dad said, hoarsely. "At least . . . thank goodness you're safe, Helen."

In his mind I saw it all, the despair of last night—and his guilt for allowing me to escape from the house. *His* guilt! As if there was any reason for that! Hadn't Dad done everything he could to keep me safe? What had I done? I'd left behind a wounded boy who'd called out to me from the edge of his life . . .

I told Dad everything. I cried all the way through it—

couldn't stop myself—and Dad did what I suppose all dads do when their daughter is falling to pieces next to them. He sat there and racked his brains for whatever he needed to say to hold me together. But I'd had plenty of opportunity to consider what had taken place back there in the storm. Not even Dad could convince me that I'd behaved decently. I knew the truth.

"I deserted him," I said. "That's what I did. Milo needed so much, and I just left him there."

"No, that's not what happened at all," Dad answered sharply. "That's just nonsense. You did everything you could for Milo, Helen. You even walked at night through a storm to reach him! And when you got there, faced with the thing you saw . . . well, anyone would have reacted the same way."

"*You* wouldn't have," I said. "You'd never have left him out there."

"Yes," he said firmly, "I would."

"I don't believe you, Dad."

I looked away from him, and for a while Dad simply held me.

"You trusted Milo," he said. "Then what did he do? He showed you a kind of . . . monster."

I considered that. Was Milo a monster? I'd certainly fled from him as if he was a kind of monster. When he lay in Coldharbour's dirt with his hands falling apart, and saw me run, I wonder what Milo thought of me?

Dad said, "Look at me, Helen." I glanced up, not quite

able to meet his eyes. "You didn't leave the boy alone," he said. "Walter's back there with him. And not only Walter. The twins and Thomas —"

"I still deserted him, Dad."

"Stop blaming yourself for everything," he said, angry now. "You didn't ask for any of this! That boy! How dare he! You *didn't* make any conscious decision to abandon Milo, or anything like it. You were . . . you were just scared out of your wits, that's all! For goodness sake, Helen, that's all that happened!"

"He was . . . he looked so terrible!" I yelled, suddenly bursting into tears again. "I couldn't stand it, all that pain pouring out of him! I couldn't!"

Dad held me tightly. "No one could have. Whatever he's becoming, it's frightening. What do we really know about Milo? Didn't you say Thomas was afraid as well, the moment he saw him? Maybe he had a good reason to be!" Dad paused, then said slowly, "Do you know something, Helen, I don't think you abandoned Milo at all. I'm being completely truthful with you now. It seems to me that you stayed longer than most people would ever have done. You stayed until you started to burn. How can you ask more of yourself than that?"

I let Dad go on, finding myself clinging desperately to his reassurances. "The boy misled you," Dad murmured, stroking my hair. "At the very least, he did that. He gave you no warning about what he would look like, or how much he was suffering."

Misled me? Had Milo really done that?

"No," I said. "Milo didn't hide his pain from me. The truth is, in my mind I had a picture of a golden boy. When I ran through the storm to be with him I'd hoped for . . ."

I knew what I'd hoped for. Despite Milo's pain, I'd still expected a smile, some hint of affection. I'd expected him to walk up to me on two normal legs, take my hand and show me a kind of miracle.

"I abandoned him," I said.

"You left Milo with other children who will do their best for him!"

"If they hadn't been there, I'd still have run. Even when Walter gave me a second chance to help, I didn't take it. I ran from that as well."

Dad stared at me. "I'm glad you did!" he said fiercely. "Otherwise, you might not be here now."

I said nothing to that. For a while we simply sat there, wrestling with our emotions. But there was one more thing Dad had to know. "Unless he gets help," I said, "I think . . . Milo's going to die."

"Oh, Helen . . ."

The thought of any child suffering tore Dad apart, but his overriding concern was still to protect me. He'd already considered getting the police involved, but what kind of report would they believe? A bald-headed boy, sir, with golden skin, and there might be a couple of insectivore girls and a giant hanging about nearby? Yes, sir, naturally we'll commit all our forces . . .

"Dad," I said, "Milo is not going to survive unless we do something for him."

Dad gazed at me. What he wanted to do was lock me in, bolt every window and door in the house and stand guard outside. But he also suspected that I'd find a way to slip away. He didn't want that to happen. I felt the struggle inside. Then he came to a decision.

"We'll go together to find him."

I hadn't expected this, and clutched him, suddenly realizing how much I'd wanted Dad to say it.

"I've got a condition," he said. "You get some sleep first." He stopped my objections. "If you're going to be any use to this boy of yours, you need it. Just a few hours." He was right. Now that I was safely home, I could hardly keep my eyes open. "Come on," Dad said. He helped me to my room and closed the curtains. After I got into bed, he pulled the quilt around my shoulders and smoothed it out. "I'll be in the guest room again," he said. "If you need anything, just shout." *I love you.*

"I love you too, Dad."

A look of surprise creased his face, then he smiled broadly. "We're going to get through this, Helen," he said. "And we'll do the right thing for Milo, too. I promise."

Dad locked my door. He felt awful about it, but that didn't stop him—he still didn't completely trust me. I thought I'd never sleep, but I was so exhausted that I think only a new scream from Milo could have woken me. No scream came. In the late afternoon, when my eyes finally opened, I lay there perversely wishing for that scream, anything to prove that Milo was still alive.

Half the food in the house seemed to be on the table when I came downstairs. "I've eaten," Dad said. "This lot's for you; take your pick. I've packed other food, and got our walking gear ready. Whatever else happens, Helen, we'll be prepared for any conditions Coldharbour has to throw at us."

We left the house shortly afterwards. Dad drove the car to the southern edge of the town. From there we would have to make our way on foot—any usable roads into Coldharbour had long disappeared. I stopped for a moment to peer beyond the bridge linking us with the mud flats. All I could see was mile after mile of steel girders and derelict huts that looked alike. Only the refuse dumps, standing out like peaks against Coldharbour's flatness, offered something to aim for.

We crossed the river, and as we did I wondered what I was doing. Even with Dad beside me, I didn't feel ready to confront Milo again. Hadn't he terrified me before? If he was still transforming, his pain might be worse. Wouldn't I run again? Probably, I thought. But at least I'm going to find you. Even without your screams, I'll find you, Milo.

The sun was already low in the sky by the time Dad and I set off into Coldharbour. Only Milo was capable of sending his thoughts from long distances, but one gang boy, walking home, was close enough for me to dip into his mind. The boy did not know where Milo was, but he'd heard of a giant, and had once seen Emily streaking across the landscape.

I let his mind lead me to that place.

In the fading light, surrounded by rats competing with seagulls for the choicest of the leftovers, we arrived at the heart of the northern dump. Dad and I climbed up the lower slopes of rubbish. From the summit, out of breath, we screened our eyes from the wind.

"There's still a long way to go," I said.

"Do you know which direction, Helen?"

"Yes—come on." Helping each other, we picked our way across the dump. By the time we were off, the seagulls were screeching and wheeling in the sky, preparing to return to their roosting nests further up the coast.

Above their screeches, dominating everything else, was another sound. I'd grown used to it. Endlessly there, eternally gnawing away, it was the sound I had come to hate and dread—the sound of the roar. Only this time it was different. This time the roar seemed to break free and suddenly burst over me.

It came loudly from all directions, like a mouth next to my face.

"What is it?" Dad asked, holding me up. "Helen!"

But I hardly heard his words. The world seemed to tilt and fall away as my gift reached out. It reached out like it had done for Milo, but this time it went much farther, raced beyond the dumps, beyond Coldharbour, beyond all adults and children, beyond our world entirely, until at last it located something. It found the source of the roar.

It glimpsed the roarer.

Not human, not animal. Vaster. There was nothing on our world to compare the roarer with because it was larger than our world. Its stomach alone was larger—and it was starving. I sensed its long thick body moving through space, feeding on the particles of matter there, and needing more. That was why it screamed. It was hunger that made it roar.

My mind drew back, unable to stand even this brief contact. But I did not withdraw soon enough. The roarer stopped. Just for a moment it paused, sensing me. Perhaps it smelled me, even across the immense distances of space. Then it moved on again between the stars, surer than it had been of its destination. It dragged its famished body towards us more urgently.

Dad was shouting at me, trying to bring me back. I felt his hands on me, shaking me, and at last I let out a scream of my own.

"Helen, what's happening? Tell me what to do! Tell me . . ."

I looked at Dad, and though I could see his lips forming words they were being drowned out. The only sound I could hear in the world was the roar. Barely able to speak, I pressed Dad to move on. I clutched his hand, and together we ran towards Milo and the setting sun.

FIFTEEN

the river

THOMAS

Throughout the day I'd been sweating inside a fever. While it gripped me, I was clearly aware of only one thing—the roar. The sinister quality of it never left us now. Even my dreams were filled with the nightmare of it. And the slow-beating wing—the one note of hope we all clung to—had faded almost to nothingness.

I slept most of the day. While I did so the twins worked tirelessly to hold Milo together. In those brief times I knew what was happening around me, their busy hands were always doing something for him. And he seemed to appreciate it. At least, when the twins offered him a bite to eat or put a cup to his lips, he smiled as if he really understood their kindness. Once I woke to see him smiling up at Freda as if she was a saint.

"If I'd more to give," she murmured softly to him, "I'd give it."

"If I'd more to give," Emily said, "I'd love 'im with it."

The twins took care of me, too, though I wondered if Walter needed their help more. He'd always taken on too much responsibility, our Walter, it was just part of his nature, but it was awful to see him looking so miserable. All those muscles, but what could he do for Milo? What could any of them do?

Only my beauty was keeping Milo alive. There was precious little left of it. Perhaps I should have been more nervous about that, but what Milo had said to me earlier had changed my mind about many things. I trusted him more. The purpose of my beauty seemed clearer to me now: to lessen Milo's suffering while he finished his transformation. I couldn't be sure, but more and more the power lifting out of me and into him felt like a natural thing.

Most of the time, though, I was too wrapped up in my own pain to notice anything going on around me. Whatever had struck me down, I felt worse than ever. My throat ached; my eyes burned; the smallest gulps of air were difficult. Milo would moan, and usually I'd follow him up straightaway with a haggard breath of my own—nearly as long and loud—with the twins anxiously flitting between us all the while. I'd never realized you could have pain in so many places at once! Every part of my body was racked by some dull or stabbing grief.

When I did wake up, it was the stench I noticed. Milo absolutely stank of decay. I could smell him all over me, an odor so bad I couldn't even identify it.

Shortly before sunset, I woke to whisperings in the

shack. When I heard my name mentioned, I kept my eyes half-shut.

" . . . all wasting away, Toms is," Emily was saying. "Oh, it ain't right not to say! We got to!"

"But ee'll go berserk!" Freda replied. "Oo knows what ee'll do?" She sounded like a lost soul. "Oh, no, what am I saying? Course we 'ave to tell 'im. Course we do, Emms!"

I remained as still as I could, waiting for more.

"Walts, what do you think?" Freda asked.

All this time Walter had been glancing agonizingly between me and Milo—as if he didn't know who needed his help most. Now he shuffled his feet, and said in an undertone, "He's l-looking the s-same, isn't he? Like Milo did when we f-first saw him. Don't t-tell Tommy y-yet. I'm go-going to get h-help."

"Oo's help?"

"Helen. She m-might understand. She knows th-things about Milo we d-don't."

"Helen was scared stiff of 'im, more like!" Freda said. "She'll never come here unless you make her."

"I won't n-need to m-make her," Walter said. "She'll c-come if I *ask* her." He looked at the twins, obviously trying to convince himself. He started to rise, then changed him mind. "Nah, nah," he said. "C-can't leave you on your own. Too m-much happening."

"No, Walts," Freda told him. "If you think Helen might be able to help, you go. Toms has been asleep ages. I doubt ee'll wake."

Walter hesitated a moment more. "W-w-won't be long, then," he said, putting on his patchwork jacket, and giving Freda his smile.

"Good," she whispered. "Don't be."

I shut my eyes tight as Walter hovered briefly next to me. Then he left the shack. As soon as I could no longer hear his footsteps, I fully opened my eyes. Emily gazed back at me, trying to work out how long I might have been listening.

"You all right, are yer, Toms?" she said, as casually as she could. "Feeling a bit better, eh?"

"Never mind that," I answered. "What exactly did Walter mean just now when he said I looked like Milo?" With an effort I propped myself up. "Why wasn't I told anything? Well?"

The twins stared at me fearfully, tears suddenly starting in their eyes. "It's all right," I said, mistaking the meaning of their expressions. "I won't go berserk, whatever it is. Come on—just tell me what Walter meant."

There was a shuffling movement, and I turned to see Milo.

He sat comfortably on my old mattress, sipping water. He was able to hold the cup himself now; he didn't need assistance from the twins. His arms were still hard against his chest, but his skin had altered. Beneath the golden skin hanging in tatters there were several points of silver. They lit up the shack like stars.

"Milo . . . " I said, finding a smile from somewhere.

"You look . . . far better . . . you . . . "

I trailed off when I noticed that he was wearing one of my shirts. I don't know why that unnerved me, but it did. He stared at me strangely. He stared at me just like the twins, and just like them there were tears in his eyes.

Suddenly I realized—all their tears were for me.

"I'm all right," I said automatically. "Aren't I?"

I looked at my hand. All the flesh was pasty white. I lifted it to my nose and the reek of rotting flesh shuddered through me. All along, I'd been smelling my own decay!

"What?" I screamed, trying to get up. My left leg wouldn't move properly. I threw the blankets off, and when I prodded my knee the flesh felt dead.

Emily screamed. She actually screamed. Freda held her hands over her mouth.

I got up—and it took every bit of energy I had. Emily rushed over to help, holding me upright. I stood there tottering like a baby, seeing how much pressure I could put on the left leg. Not much. My one good leg and Emily were the only things keeping me from collapsing. I hadn't looked at the rest of my body yet; I didn't want to. "What . . . what do I look like?" I asked.

The girls wouldn't answer, either because they were so upset or because it was too hard to describe.

"Sit down, Tommy," Freda was saying. "We're . . . we're gonna w-work this out."

"Walts will be back soon," Emily added.

"What's he going to do?" I demanded. "Bring crutches? You think that'll make everything better?"

"You stay calm," Emily implored me.

I tried. I still hadn't examined the rest of my body. They were all doing enough of that for me! No, I had to look, stop panicking, face it. How bad could it be?

"Just relax, Toms," Emily was saying. "Sit yerself down on the sheet there."

"Will you just shut up!" I screamed. "Shut up!" I was trembling, trembling. "Get me a mirror!" I ordered Freda.

"You don't want to see, Toms," she said.

"Yes, I do. Get the mirror!"

"We ain't got one."

"In your bag!" I shouted. "I know you've got one. Get it or I swear I'll . . . I don't know what I'll do!"

Emily glanced at Freda, then went to the back of the shack. Inside the pocket of a bag there was a small rectangular mirror, smudged with the girls' fingerprints.

Freda begged me to sit. I took the mirror and lifted it— not to my face, though, not yet; I looked down, angling it to show off my body first. I should have known what I'd see in that mirror. My symptoms were hardly new. Milo. I looked like Milo—but not the new version of him. No, I looked exactly like the old one, the hot-skinned one with all the bits of flesh hanging off. Only the gold was missing. I raised the mirror to my face. I touched my left eyelid and it slid away painlessly. I moistened my lips and they hissed ever so softly. My bald head almost shone. My hair lay all over the bedclothes.

"What . . . what have you done to me?" I croaked at Milo. He said nothing. I looked at Emily and Freda, and they looked back at me, tears and love in their eyes.

"You did this!" I screamed at Milo.

I wanted to smash him. But more than that I wanted to know . . . why? Hadn't he blessed me for what I'd done for him? Hadn't he given me thanks for the kindness of my beauty? "How . . . could you do this?" I said. "How could you?"

He sat up on my mattress, gazing at me with an expression I couldn't understand at all.

The twins gazed in horror at the state of me. "You—you weren't anywhere near this bad before," Emily murmured. "Oh, Toms . . . "

Milo hadn't taken his eyes off me. "Good-looking, aren't I!" I shouted. Suddenly I felt a stomach pain—and realized my beauty was in its last spasm. Yet even now, with it gasping out of me, Milo took what was left, siphoning the final dregs for himself. Then he flinched— and his heart boomed out like a cannon. With reckless movements of his bloodied fingers, he started tearing at the shreds of his skin. What was underneath flashed silver. One flash. Another. Another. Each one nearly blinded us, and with every one of them my stomach howled with pain.

"That's enough! Get in the back! To the back of the

shack!" I screamed at the twins. I dragged my body towards Milo.

Freda scrambled across, took up a stance beside him. "Thomas!" she said in a commanding voice. "Thomas, you will stop this! You will stop doing this at once, do yer hear me!"

"For mercy's sake, Toms! . . . " Emily begged.

But for once my beauty came to my aid. My terror was so great that it gave me the last shudders of its strength, enough to catch the twins and tie them up, enough at least to haul myself over to Milo and gaze into his eyes. His healthy, richly silver eyes. The lids had returned. It was only my lids that were missing now. He batted his own at me. I gripped his arm, wanting to hear it break. "So you're trying to kill me, eh? You *are* trying to kill me, after all! We'll see about that!"

"Wait," Freda was saying. "Toms, listen to uz!"

"No!" I shouted back.

I tested Milo's heaviness. He weighed very little, and as I picked him up he made no attempt to resist me. Instead, raising his still-bandaged hands, he stroked my face.

"More affection? Still pretending?" I screamed at him. "A tiny bit more beauty to drain out, is there?" His skin flashed urgently silver again, and I yelped in pain. "Trying to finish your transformation, eh? Why don't you give me that saintly smile and bless you Tommy routine? It worked before! Go on!"

Freda and Emily, cringing with terror, pleaded with me, but I'd stopped listening.

Milo said nothing. Gritting my teeth, I put him over my shoulder like a sack and left the shack. Sunset. I had no clear idea what I was going to do with Milo until I saw the river. Then I knew. A few gang kids had heard the commotion, and come out to see what was going on, but I didn't care. Let them watch! They wouldn't stop me. Nothing would stop me.

The twins' hysterical voices trailed away behind.

I made it at last to the river. As I put my bare foot in the water, steam hissed from my skin in the same way it had done from Milo when we first saw him. I heaved him round to face me. "I believed you!" I shrieked. "Look what you've done to me!"

I waded up to my knees, then a little further. How deep did I need to go? Milo didn't resist me. He merely continued to stroke my face, the end of my beauty still shooting into him.

"How dare you!" I screamed.

I dumped him into the river. Maybe if he'd stopped touching me, I might have had a change of heart. Maybe if he'd just put out his hands for help, or said something, *especially* if he'd said something, I might have. I don't know. I might at least have listened. But Milo didn't do any of those things. His mouth opened and closed hideously. His fingers slid from my face and he fell like a stone, sinking beneath the water. There were a few bubbles, then nothing from him. Briefly, further down-stream, I saw his body surface, as the strong current of the river raised him up. Then he sank again, and didn't reappear.

I turned and walked out of the river shallows. For some reason I was crying. Ridiculous—wasn't it good that I'd killed him? Milo. I hated that name! He didn't deserve any name! He was a parasite—parasite boy! I'd trusted him, given him everything, and look what he'd done to me!

I waited ten full minutes, to make sure that he was dead.

Then I made my way back to the shack.

SIXTEEN

the shack

HELEN

With Dad alongside me, I ran across Coldharbour.

It was a moonless night, dark. Somewhere in that darkness Milo was tumbling across the riverbed, holding on to a final breath. From that breath he reached out to me. With all his mind Milo did it, and in that moment all I could do was clutch on to Dad because I wasn't ready. I thought I would be. I'd prepared myself. All the way here I'd readied myself for more of Milo's pain, but this was more than physical pain. It was anguish.

And it was not for himself. It was for Thomas.

Dad ran along the riverbank, looking over the water for any sign of a struggling boy. Seeing nothing, he removed his jacket and shoes, trying to estimate how deep he would have to dive. "Is Milo here?" he called out, taking lungfuls of air. "Helen, answer me!"

I looked at the storm-swollen river. Dad was a good swimmer, but I doubted even he could take on a current this strong. "Wait," I said.

Milo, I thought—where are you? And I felt him stir. From the murk of the river bottom, two fingers scrabbled, trying to get above the water. But he couldn't reach high enough—and even if he had been able to, I would never have seen his fingers in the darkness.

"Helen," Dad said, "who else knows where he is?"

Of course. One person knew exactly where he had dumped Milo into the river. I focused my mind on Thomas, and found him. He was in the shack, lying on the floor between the twins. They were desperately trying to hold his body together, but Thomas was barely aware of their efforts because he was in torment.

To kill someone. To have done that. To have had a life in your arms, one you nurtured for so long, and then to have let that life slip away. And then to have waited until you were certain that life was utterly extinguished. Thomas wasn't a killer, but he'd left Milo to drown, and even now he was trying to make sense of what had happened in their final moments together.

Dad and I followed the path of Thomas's mind to the shack.

"I'm going in first," Dad said. "Stay here."

The shack door was partially open. A tiny amount of starlight illuminated the scene.

Thomas lay there. The state of him was so appalling that Dad instinctively tried to block the sight from me. I pushed past, ready at least for this. Apart from the gold,

Thomas looked exactly like the version of Milo who had crawled out of the darkness. The twins were draped across him, Emily cradling his face as if she could hold it together by sheer willpower. She gazed up at me. "Helen, please help uz."

It was all in her mind, the way Thomas had stumbled back to the shack, forlornly calling out their names. Since then the twins had devoted themselves to him, but their care was not enough because in the end Emily and Freda only had hands, and even such skillful hands as theirs did not have the capacity to reach down inside Thomas's failing lungs to repair them.

"Drowned 'im," Emily murmured to me. "How could yer do it to 'im, Toms? Oh, how could yer?" She glared down as if she was about to strike him, then sobbed instead, nestling her face against his shoulder.

From the floor Thomas stared defiantly at me. That stare! Like Milo's in the storm! He raised his lidless eyes.

"See this!" he screamed. "Do you *see!*" The skin fell away from part of his face. He tore at another flap hanging from his cheek. "Look at what Milo's done!" He dragged himself across the floor. Dad came between us, but I said no, and allowed Thomas to come forward. Before he could reach me, though, I heard footsteps approaching the shack.

There was no mistaking that great tread across the earth.

"Walts!" Freda wailed, glancing frantically at us. "Ee

can't see Thomas like this! What'll it do to 'im?"

She tried pushing the door shut with her foot. Walter, of course, would not allow that. He entered the shack, moving her leg gently aside. One by one Walter carefully checked us, his fingers running lightly over our bodies, convincing himself we were unharmed. Then he made himself look at Thomas—and I screamed, because it wasn't possible to be in Walter's mind at that moment without screaming.

"It weren't your fault!" Freda cried out, pressing herself fiercely against him.

"No, Walts!" Emily said. "You weren't to know, how could yer! Come here to me!"

"Oh . . . oh . . . " Walter's face caved in. He couldn't accept what he was seeing. Emily and Freda held him, trying to explain, but Walter kept just shaking his head and grinding his hands into the floor. "I w-w-was m-m-meant to p-protect . . . " He kissed Thomas. "What good . . . what g-good am I if I c-c-can't d-do, even d-do . . . " He trailed off. He slumped to the floor, turning his face away from us in shame.

Thomas reached out to me. He gripped my ankle. He was trying to talk. There was really too much pain in his throat to talk, but Thomas had no choice. He had to ask, because surely if anyone could understand it was me. "Milo . . . didn't he deserve what I did to him?" he said. "I *trusted* him! A meal, that's all I was! Just a thing to feed off, until he was ready. All of us—freaks for his

needs! Tell the twins, Helen! They're still convinced by
Milo's act! But you know! When you first saw him you
ran! Tell—"

I held his shoulders. "Thomas, stop. Listen to me—"

"No! *You* listen!" he cried, tears coursing down his face.
"I couldn't run like you! I wasn't capable, was I? He—"

"He's alive," I said.

The twins gazed at me. Thomas shook his head. "I
made certain . . . "

"He is *still* alive!" I shouted.

Thomas's mouth twisted sideways.

"I should have understood," I said. "That first time
we saw him, I should. But I was too frightened to look
properly. Like you, I was scared of him. Thomas, Milo
never meant to harm you. He needed your beauty,
that's all. It was the only thing keeping him alive
through all the changes. And he took so much pain on
himself. He never passed the worst of it onto you, only
a small part . . . "

Thomas hauled himself away from me. After what he'd
done, he was willing to accept almost anything except
this. "Get out!" he shrieked. "Did you hear me? Get out!"

I followed him across the room, kneeling beside him.
"It's not your fault," I whispered. "All that pain, I know
what it was like. When I saw Milo, I ran. Thomas, it was
you who stayed!"

Walter stirred. He gently folded Thomas's face inside
his hands. "Don't y-you see?" he cried. "You c-couldn't

bear it, that's all. Of c-course not, Tommy! Are you l-listening to H-Helen? You c-couldn't b-bear it, but you did! All this t-time it was only you k-keeping Milo alive! Only you!"

Thomas tried to get to his feet. "I'll . . . I'll . . . " He broke down in tears, clutching at Freda. "Help me," he pleaded. "I'll . . . I'll take you there . . . to the river . . . " When his feet would not budge, he raised his arms for Walter to lift him.

Walter started to do so, then stopped. He turned his head sharply, staring at the door of the shack. And then we all did the same, because something was coming. Even Dad felt it coming: a power, a force, a crescendo moving towards us at tremendous speed.

Beauty.

Like a fullness of wind all the beauty Thomas had given Milo swept past us. It sought out its owner and, in a single huge wave, swept inside him.

Thomas lay there, panting in wonder, restored. His hands were his own again, his lungs at ease, his face cool, unblemished.

But there was no time for us to dwell on this, because what followed the beauty was a scream. It came from the river. Milo, I knew, had held on for as long as he could, but now his mouth was opening in the water.

Thomas shouted, "Walter!"

Without hesitation Walter scooped Thomas up. He placed me and Dad onto his shoulders. Emily and Freda scrambled to find places on his legs. Thomas bent to whisper and, protecting our faces, Walter smashed his way out of the shack and ran.

SEVENTEEN

the clamor

MILO

Milo lay on the riverbed, waiting to drown.

His lungs were larger than before, and the last snatch of air he had managed to take as Thomas dumped him under the water had sustained him for many minutes. But now that air was nearly gone. While he still could, Milo tried to crawl out. The current, too strong, bore his body up; the swell took him downstream.

Eyes, he thought, guide me now.

But the turbulent river threw up too much silt for him to find a way back to the bank.

As he drifted, he thought about beauty. When Thomas had carried him to the water, Milo had tried to speak to him, but his throat had changed too much. He could only open and close his mouth, a sight that appalled Thomas. Now, distantly, Milo sensed the heavy tread of Walter. He heard the thoughts of Helen, imploring him to hold on.

Too late, he thought. They could not arrive in time.

In time for what?

Milo looked down at himself. Even now, clinging to a final lung's breath, his body continued to change. The tatters of golden skin were ripping away. The main muscles of his arms were fused like welded steel to his ribs. The bandages had fallen from his hands, and the bones of his fingers had lengthened.

And his heart howled. It was a bigger heart, almost tearing from his chest.

Milo stared at the river bottom, and saw the murk all lit up silver. Where before the silver had escaped only between the cracks of his skin, now it pushed adamantly through. His legs shone. Fish hid from the light of his face. His shoulders glowed—and split. Silver gushed out, and behind the light something else struggled out of his back to be born.

Milo tried desperately to hold on to life. He clamped his mouth shut to avoid taking a breath. For a moment he stayed entirely still, lowering his head, attempting to survive on a last ebb of air. Every part of his will held back from taking that first gasp which would fill him with water.

But his body knew it must breathe. Eventually it would take a breath.

Just before it did, Milo heard a sound. It was not Walter or the others, not the sound of children at all. It was an immenseness, a depth, a roaring out of rage that represented the frenzied tearing up of the entire world.

And Milo understood something at last: he understood that he was meant to lead the defense against the roarer. He was the first of the guardians. He was the forerunner, the outrider, the first. Like Thomas, like Helen, like Walter and the twins, he was the first to emerge and stand against it.

Too late. He had understood too late. Could the others build a fortress on their own? No.

I'm dying, he thought. He tried to calm himself so that he could perform one last duty. All this time he had held on to Thomas's beauty, but now it was time to let it return. Since he would die anyway, he would at least do this one small thing.

Like a caress Milo felt all the beauty rise out of his heart.

And, afterwards, there was no dignified ending of life. There was only panic. Milo opened his mouth to take a breath—and the water entered. He screamed once, then even his screams were cut off as the river filled his throat. And filled his lungs. And filled his kidneys and his arms.

All pain was gone. With the entry of the water it ended. His throat opened out. It made a final alteration and, as if his mouth were a hole in the world, the river rushed inside him. The final golden shreds of skin fell away. He was bright with silver.

There was a clamor from his back, a rustle he could not see.

EIGHTEEN

the silver child

THOMAS

Walter ran, and to anyone watching from the night gangs we must have been something to behold: me under his arm, Helen and her dad perched on his shoulders, with the twins clinging to the flares of Walter's jeans. Not that any of us cared what we looked like.

Milo alive—I shuddered to think of that.

What kind of a boy could have survived what I'd done? And if we found him on time, what would I say? What words would I have?

As we neared the river I tried to remember where I'd carried Milo in, but there was no need. Freda was pointing at the night sky. Above the river, it shimmered silver. The undersides of clouds were lit up. Seagulls, mistaking the silver for dawn, were flying sleepily out of the west. And then we heard more birds, whole families of them taking flight from the river itself, disturbed by a sound.

A heartbeat.

A single wild boom of heartbeat that stopped us cold.

"Walter," I said, clutching him, "take us away from here!"

"No, n-no," he said. "It's—"

A second boom. A third—faster, sending a spray off the river.

The twins and I tried to scramble from Walter's grasp, but he held us until we were calm enough to follow his instructions. After what had happened before, I thought Walter would never let me out of his arms again, but he told me to reposition myself on his back, so that at least his hands were free to defend us. The twins slid round to the back of his legs. Then, with all of us clinging on, Walter took a few more cautious strides towards the riverbank.

There we waited, while the heartbeat grew in volume.

The reverberations of that heart! The passion of it!

And with it kicking its life inside him, Milo emerged from the river.

I had no measure for the nature of child arising from the darkness. Milo's scalp alone, as he lifted it, covered a third of the river. Beneath it the waters had no choice other than to rise with him, rise upward on the dimensions of his features. The span of his face! The breadth of his shoulders! His neck rose like a tower. The proportions of his chest filled the river.

In that first moment we were all scared, and I think we might have run, except that Milo himself seemed so perturbed by his own condition. He knelt timidly in the river, as if he did not trust his legs to carry him. He glanced uncertainly at his arms. They were now entirely attached to his chest—the bones fused against his ribs, like buttresses for a greater weight to come. Only his hands were still free to move. Each of the fingers was elongated, a thin bone without flesh. Unsure of himself, Milo moved with great care. He placed his finger-bones across both banks of the river, helping his legs take him to his full height.

And now the river was not even deep enough to cover his ankles. When Milo turned his head, clouds broke against the resistance of his ears. He stood in profile to us, and we saw the North Star in the gap between his lips.

Nevertheless he stood shakily, as if he still might fall.

All this while Helen had been clinging to Walter, gazing up. "He looks like the wonder I expected to meet that first time," she said. "He's the boy I wanted."

"A silver child," Freda murmured.

I looked at Milo. I'd seen gold on him before, and glints of something else, but now every surface of his body was a sheen of lustrous silver. He was so radiant that I wondered how we could look upon him at all. It was, I thought, as if our eyes had been waiting for him. I glanced across at Helen, and saw she felt the same way.

Dawn arrived, the sun creeping over the humps of the eastern dump, but we barely noticed. All the light in the world seemed meaningless next to Milo. The twins peered between Walter's legs.

"If I was the moon," Emily murmured, "I'd disappear."

"If I was the sun," Freda said, her arm around her, "I'd shed a tear."

For a while Milo simply towered over us, gazing outward across Coldharbour. Then he turned to stare at the ground. His eyes were so large that it was not possible to gauge precisely where he was looking, or at whom. But I knew. I knew he was looking at me.

I'd been hoping for a miracle. I'd hoped Milo had become so *different* that what had happened before between us would not matter anymore—or that he would not remember. But as his eyes curved to the ground, I knew he remembered.

He understood exactly what I had done to him.

Should I run? Walter would take me if I asked, and perhaps the power of his legs would carry me halfway across Coldharbour before Milo reacted.

But that would not be far enough.

Milo lifted his foot. The shadow of it rose above me like a mountain. I shrank against Walter, thinking Milo was going to crush me. But Milo stepped backwards. A single stride took him across the river. Another step and both his feet were on the boundary of Coldharbour, their weight flattening the slopes of the northern dump.

From there Milo lowered himself to the ground. He lay flat, on his chest. He placed his head near the river. The heaviness of his chin striking the mud flats buried his face nearly up to the lips. His eyes, staring at me, were larger than my body.

I stood shaking in front of him, trying to say something.

"The river . . . " I managed. "When I carried you, dropped you . . . I didn't—" I broke off, unable to finish. I wanted to say more; I struggled to, but Milo shook his head, no, no, no need for that.

He moved his own lips. It was still difficult for him, and his words, when they reached me, came like a wind.

"Thomas," he said, "forgive me."

Forgive *him*? I gazed up.

"I gave you no choice," Milo said. "Yet you kept me alive. Even when you believed you were dying, you did that."

"I was frightened—"

"Because I took everything from you." There were tears in Milo's eyes. They were normal tears; they fell down his face without drying, like our tears. He lifted one of his silver hands, as if to cup my face inside his fingers. Then he stood again, rising in stages. His face, once it reached the clouds, remained still, as if listening intently.

"Can you hear it?" he whispered. "Can you?"

And, of course, we could. It was the roar, ever closer now—as if with the emergence of Milo it was seeking us all out.

"Soon everyone will hear," Milo said. "I do not know what it is, only that it means to consume us. It is an appetite, a hunger. That is all the roar knows, perhaps all it will ever need to know to hunt us down. Yet there may still be time to prevent it."

His eyes looked through ours, and when he spoke again his voice had the weight of empires. "I am the first of the defenders," he declared. "I am the herald, the harbinger, the first. Prepare yourselves to meet those who are yet to come." Then, looking at each of us, he thundered:

"ARE YOU READY?"

We recoiled in shock. Only Helen seemed to know what Milo meant, and she was more apprehensive than all of us.

"I . . . think whatever makes the roar . . . " she said weakly, "I've helped it. I've helped it discover us. I didn't mean to, but when I looked into its mind . . . "

"No," Milo said, "it would have found us just the same." He turned gravely to her. "I suffered pain," he said. "I never believed, Helen, you would walk willingly towards so much pain. Yet you did, and did so alone. Many from the next generation of children will also be alone. Some will not be able to express what they need. But you will know what to do for them. You will."

Helen shook her head fearfully. "I . . . won't. I'm not ready . . . for whatever it is."

"You think you are not strong enough?"

"I'm not."

"You are."

Milo returned his gaze to me. "The work for your

beauty is only beginning," he said. "Are you ready, Thomas?"

I shook my head, not understanding, but Milo glanced nervously at the sky, as if a greater duty already beckoned him there. He said one more thing:

"Walter! Protect them all!"

And then, gathering himself, Milo took a deep breath. He arched his back. He raised what was left of his hands, and the bones stretched into a cord-like thinness. Each cord lashed the air, then reached eagerly behind, until there was an unfurling of something stronger and heavier than feathers.

Wings.

Five times the span of Milo's body were each of the wings, and on them he beat a path into the sky. The motion created a storm of wind that knocked us to our knees. Milo soared upward, in long hesitant arcs, and all around us paper and plastic and anything not anchored to the ground rose from the rubbish dumps of Coldharbour, dancing in the air.

With our hair blowing into our eyes, we watched.

Milo's first movements upward had been almost clumsy. But soon he gained a greater understanding of the power of his wings, and when at last he opened them fully nothing was the same. Their extent hid the stars. Gulls cried out, frightened by the noise of their beating. Whole towns fell under their shadow. Clouds were swept aside. A backward thrust of one wing, hanging over the sea, created a wave that started on the shore and forged like the beginning of a new ocean away from the land.

A beautiful, loud, complete silverness enveloped us.

For a moment Milo hovered uncertainly, as if he was not sure himself that the wings would carry his great bulk any higher. Then he laughed, and was sure, and took up a position in the upper reaches of the sky. He held that position—centered over Coldharbour—and looked calmly in all directions, his wings now beating to the same slow steady rhythm.

I recognized that rhythm. I stared at Freda and saw that she, too, recognized the sound of it.

"The wing," she whispered. "It was Milo, Toms. Not just the roar. Somehow we were hearing Milo, too . . . "

I looked up from Walter's arms, and from this distance I could see that Milo was not merely a silver child. He glowed other hues of color as well. I don't even know what colors they were, all colors, drifting down his body in a gradual way, like clouds over mountains. And even as we watched the purity of light grew, until his eyes— rimmed with bronze and dipped with fierceness—were almost unbearable.

Milo turned to face the world. Defying anything to resist him, he gazed across the town—and beyond it. We looked, and saw that everywhere lights were being switched on, windows thrown wide, doors opened.

"Children," Helen whispered.

Milo drew them. His size, his light, called out to them.

He was a beacon, a summons commanding them to come together where he could defend them.

The first children were not long arriving. Initially a scattering of them were just distant silhouettes across Coldharbour, bathed in Milo's silverness. Then I saw that the silhouettes belonged to boys, members of night gangs who must have been out patrolling their territories.

"They can hear the roar," Helen said to me. "It's not just us anymore. All children can hear it, now."

The first to stagger towards us was a young girl with a doll. She wore a dressing gown and I think she must have been traveling for some time to have reached us so soon. The rubbish of Coldharbour had still not settled from Milo's early wingbeats, and as the girl made her way towards us a newspaper blew across her face. She pulled it off. Seeing us, she hesitated—then raised her face to stare at the sky.

"Milo," she said—lifting her arms to him.

And Milo left his position amongst the clouds. To be with her he did that, the wind rushing ahead of him. He tried to alight on the surface, but his legs could no longer bear his weight, as if they were never meant to. Instead, Milo maintained a place just above her and delicately lifted the soil under the girl. He held her in the palm of his hand, and kissed her.

"Jenny," he murmured.

She stayed there for a long time, curled inside a whorl of his finger.

"Safeguard her," Milo whispered at last to Walter and the twins.

Then he swept back his wings and returned to the sky, anchoring himself in the same position as before—eyes outward—his body slowly turning and turning, guiding children everywhere towards Coldharbour.

I looked up at him and some part of me realized that Milo would never leave the sky again. His task from now onward would always keep him there. He was a protector. He was a guardian, the first of the defenders, a shield forever facing in the direction from which the roar would come.

Jenny stood nearby, holding her doll. While the twins tried to coax her to approach them, Helen's dad was staring out across the mud to the south and west.

"More are coming," he said. "How many are there?"

Helen pressed his hand. "They're *all* coming. I can hear their minds."

We waited, and gradually children started to arrive from every direction, stumbling over the rubbish-strewn ground. Nearly all of them had been caught sleeping, and turned up in nightwear. They stared in awe at Milo, but also at each other.

Jenny was still the closest. She stood beside us, uncertainly twiddling her doll. Emily and Freda, hardly able to contain their excitement, climbed down from Walter, and skittered across to her. Then they stopped, got off their hands, and stood up using only their legs, trying to look more normal for Jenny.

"If I'd a grace," Freda said, "I'd charm the day."

"If I'd a song," Emily shouted out loud, "I'd sing away!"

I thought Jenny would run, hearing that shout, but instead she laughed. She was not afraid of the twins. She let them come over, and played with the buttons on their dresses briefly, but there was something else she wanted.

She headed for Walter.

Knowing what reaction children normally had to him, Walter had tried to hide his size from Jenny, crouching low somewhere behind us. Jenny threaded a path to him. She extricated herself from the clutches of the singing twins and walked up to him. She held out her arms to be picked up and Walter just looked at me, and I had no words to express the joy that spread across his face.

Above us, Milo's imperturbable eyes gazed out over the world.

"The children are coming to him," I said. "But he's so high. How can they reach him?"

"No," Helen said solemnly. "Don't you understand? They're not coming to him. They're coming to *us*." She glanced at me. "I never did anything for him, you know. Milo never needed anything from me. Everything that happened was to prepare me."

"Prepare you?"

"For this." With one arm Helen held on to her dad. With the other she indicated the thousands of children scrambling around and over the dumps. Steadily, with determination, they were walking towards us across the filth and rubbish of Coldharbour.

"I'm ready," Helen said, tears flowing from her. "And so are you."

And she was right. I looked at the singing twins, and at Walter, now with Jenny in his arms, and as I did so I felt my beauty, like an ocean filling me, already making its way towards the nearest children, ready to provide whatever they needed. Amongst them were skills and gifts I could not believe.

"Are you ready?" Helen asked me.

"Yes," I said.

Walter placed Jenny on his neck. He gathered up Helen and her dad. He let me walk up his arm. The twins dropped on all fours, and clung to his knees.

And together we turned to face the children now running towards us out of the dawn.

also by cliff mcnish:

SILVER CITY

BOOK TWO OF
THE SILVER SEQUENCE

ONE

the unearthers

THOMAS

Night, and I stood watching all the children in the world leaving their homes. For a moment the drone of an overhead surveillance plane drowned out their voices; then the plane passed by and their eager conversations and rushing footsteps could be heard again.

All those feet, running. Most children couldn't help themselves. Whatever place they came from, if they had any energy left they always ran the last stretch into Coldharbour. My time to be summoned had come earlier, but I'd been just like these other children. Not even thinking to leave a note for my parents, I'd left home and come breathlessly rushing into this place.

From a side street outside Coldharbour, I saw a teenage girl accidentally clatter into a boy.

"Sorry," she said, steadying his arm. "Are you okay?" She pointed towards the silver light ahead. "Look, we're nearly there!"

"I know," he said, grinning. "How do you feel?"

"Happy," the girl said. "Nervous, as well. A bit anyway."

"Me, too." He laughed. "But we got here, didn't we? We made it.'

"Yes. We did." The girl took his hand, and together they sprinted down the final sloping streets leading the way into Coldharbour.

Coldharbour. Until yesterday it had been little more than a seven-mile expanse of mud and rubbish dumps bordering the sea. Apart from myself and five other special children, the only things living there had been seagulls and a good supply of well-fed rats. The only people who ever disturbed the rats were a scattering of bored gang kids with nothing better to do.

Not anymore. As I gazed out over the mud, I couldn't begin to count the numbers of new children settling inside Coldharbour.

They'd been arriving all night. For hours I'd watched them running here, leaving everything they knew behind. Most weren't even properly dressed. They turned up in socks, slippers, pajamas, vests, nightgowns, T-shirts or what-ever else they'd been wearing when they received the call. Some teenagers had waited long enough to throw on coats or decent footwear before leaving home, but not many.

Attempts were being made to stop them, of course. No doubt some quick-acting parents managed to haul their own kids back indoors if they caught them in time. And as the night dragged on police units also arrived, taking up positions all around the area. In western Coldharbour army brigades had even driven in, hurriedly erecting barricades to prevent anyone crossing the roads over the river. The barricades didn't work. Children fought their way past. Naturally a few got caught, but most escaped and were soon trying to get inside again.

I knew what was happening. I knew because I'd been just the same as these other children. A few weeks earlier, I'd been determined to get here. I'd even hid on the way, hid from my own mum and dad, to make sure they wouldn't force me back home.

But, if anything, these new children seemed even more resourceful than I'd been. To get within Coldharbour they were prepared to do anything: argue, lie, join together, create a distraction—whatever they had to. It was a kind of madness, because there was nothing for us in this place: no home, no food, no shelter.

So why were we all here?

Because Milo drew us. That's all we knew. Yesterday evening, shortly after sunset, a child with a body over four miles long and with wings five times that size had appeared in the sky over Coldharbour. A vast silver-glowing child, spanning towns and the sea.

And the moment he appeared, children couldn't help

themselves: they were drawn to him. It wasn't a question of choice. There was no choice; they had to reach him.

Just after dawn the next morning, with the sun peeking over Coldharbour's eastern rubbish dumps, I stood watching a skinny little boy push through the perimeter crowds. He stumbled past me, lifting his arms skyward to be picked up. "Milo! Milo!" he called out plaintively over and over, the way all the youngsters did. "Mil-o!"

I followed the skinny boy's gaze upward. And there he was, floating at cloud level, and gleaming in the sky—Milo, the silver child.

His body-shape was like any other boy's, but that's where any resemblance to us ended. His wings left you breathless. I'd watched children walking under them for hours without reaching their end. Those colossal wings! At first I'd thought they were made of feathers, but when you judged the weight of the body they were holding up, you realized the wings couldn't possibly be made of feathers. Something better than that. Something finer. Stronger and more enduring.

With occasional flexes of the wing tips, Milo kept himself stationary. He remained in one fixed location of the sky, dead center over Coldharbour. His body lay flat and parallel to the horizon, his bare feet swaying ever so slightly, his face sometimes tilted towards us, sometimes towards the sky.

Protecting us. That's what we all felt, anyway.